Gun Jesus

James Ross

"Soldiers are dreamers."

Siegfried Sassoon

The noise no longer bothered him.
The swirling dust of an incoming storm, the sporadic report of rifle fire, the bass chittering of the .50, the stench of smoke and shit, the pop of a distant mortar followed by three or four seconds of deep fear until the crack, when it landed, somewhere else, thankfully. And the screams if someone was hit, or a moment's silence if no one was, or if they'd died instantaneously.
None of it bothered him any longer.
He thought of Rhetta and frowned; he couldn't remember her face. He thought of his parents' house and couldn't picture them living in it, only the ornaments on the mantel and the old rocking chair in the kitchen that had belonged to his grandmother. He felt a distant sadness, but no grief. He was laid up against a large rock with a through-and-through bullet wound to his right lung and no one was coming to rescue him. No Smeert team, no passing Casevac who'd land in this shitstorm of screaming 7.62mm rounds, the hot metal and eviscerating ultra-pressure waves from the mortar explosions. Who'd risk a helicopter and a whole crew to save one dying

trooper? They'd be ordered not to. They'd be right
not to. So he was dying, and he was at peace.
I wish I'd been a better man, he thought.
I wish I'd made a difference.
He thought of all the times he'd had the chance to do
the right thing and had chosen not to, had not
bothered to make a decision, or had just turned
away. He was no longer scared, only sad for the
times he had not done the right thing.

They'd held the ground, fourteen of them, down to
maybe eight still standing, and no-one without a
wound, but no matter who won or lost, he was going
to die, and he'd wasted all his chances to do the right
thing. This much was clear to him. At some point,
Luuk ran up to him to check he was still alive, fiddled
with the valve that drained out the air that was filling
his pleural cavity, and as the valve hissed, his
breathing became easier. He looked up, smiled, 'I
wish I'd been a better man, Luuk,' he said.
The medic slapped his face none too gently and
looked him in the eye, 'Don't you dare give up on me
Daan. You will survive this,' butting his helmet
against Daan's, brother to brother, 'And then you can
be any kind of man you want to be.'
Right then, a 7.62mm round hit the right side of
Luuk's helmet and punched a hole all the way
through and out through the left side, and Luuk's
eyes faded and he was gone, just a body dropped
onto the dirt. Daan flinched, tried to sit up, retching,
sweeping the blood and brains from his cheek with

disgusted fingers to get a better look at Luuk, but the weight of his wound bore down on him, smothered his breathing so that he could not move himself away from the horror. Defeated, he looked up and out across the scrub and rocks toward the hillside where the ambushers were hidden, felt a bullet skip across his body armour, felt the sandstorm growing heavier, the sky darkening and he thought, this is how it feels: darkness and storm. He almost persuaded himself it was a Valkyrie, come to take him to Valhalla, as they had done for his ancestors, and he smiled, but then he looked up again and saw that the darkness and the storm was somehow, miraculously, a helicopter that was landing no more than ten metres away from him. He saw someone lean out, shout in unmistakable English, 'Need a hand mate?' and then the man, the crew chief, dropped from the bed of the helicopter onto the ground, ignoring the gun fire that had focused on this miraculous machine, the helicopter being a far greater prize than a dozen Dutch pecekeepers, and jogged across to him, heedless of the metal that cracked and split the air around him and kicked up dust at his feet. The English soldier squatted down, grabbed Daan by the shoulders, picked him up and threw him over his shoulder like a meal sack, carrying him across to the helicopter where he rolled him onto the flat metal floor. Suddenly, with the possibility of survival, the fear and the pain came back and he cried out. The crew chief climbed in and dragged him to a sitting position against the bulkhead, and then left the chopper again. Daan watched as the crew chief ran over to Michael, the baby-faced officer, and they had a brief chat before he ran back, leapt inside, shook Daan's left shoulder reassuringly and then turned to slap the pilot on the back of the helmet, shouting 'Let's go!'

The pilot turned and shouted, 'What about the others?'

'Dead. Too many survivors to airlift. Let's go!'

Without any further discussion, the pilot twisted the throttle and the collective, and the chopper began to dust off. But after no more than ten, fifteen seconds the pilot slowed the chopper and shouted, pointing out something to the crew chief who looked out, cursed, and, leaning forward, began to argue with the pilot with much shaking of his head. Angry, he grabbed the M134 and began lighting up the hillside with three thousand rounds a minute from the minigun as the pilot set down the chopper, ripped off his own helmet and headphones, opened the door and dropped away out of sight. Moments later, the pilot reappeared shouldering a wounded talib fighter, one of the men who had been trying to kill them all, and he dumped him next to Dan. The man was alive, but his lower left leg was a tattered mess of bloodied cotton, shredded flesh and glistening bone. The crew chief shouted something at the pilot who slammed shut the door behind him and clambered forward into his seat, and they dusted off again the crew chief's minigun laid down a carpet of 5.56mm brass-jacketed ordnance towards the increasingly distant

Taliban fighters lying prone behind rocks. Daan sat back, the pain in his chest burning, his breathing increasingly difficult as the pleural cavity began to fill with air, making it increasingly difficult to breathe. He tried to catch the eye of the crew chief, but he was busy emptying the last of his ammunition into the barren hillside. Daan looked at the Taliban fighter that the pilot had risked his life to save. The man's face was white with blood loss. Daan himself could hardly breathe. He wondered if either of them would survive the flight. But he knew, if he did survive, he'd take this chance. He'd become a better man.

'Barrett!'

I turned and saw Tom Jarvis heading in my direction, a smile on his face. He took my hand and shook it vigorously. He looked pleased to see me, though we hadn't spoken in five years, and I'd only met him twice, shortly before I got involved in a three-day firefight in a remote valley in north East Afghanistan, and then again shortly before I was kicked out of the army for assaulting a Guards Colonel live on Sky TV. And when I say 'assault' it wasn't a 'stripped to the waist whilst engaging in gentlemanly fisticuffs' sort of thing, no, it was "my forehead smashed into the Colonel's face cos I couldn't be arsed to speak" type assault. At the time I'd been too exhausted to raise my fists.

'You look well,' he said, taking my arm and guiding me in the direction of the security desk.

'You look like a cultural studies professor,' I countered.

He did. Wearing chinos, a pale blue linen shirt, urban-hiking boots, his hair cut short at the collar but shaggy on top, he looked like Hugh Grant, if Hugh had spent fifteen years in an elite military unit. He signed me in and led me through the gate to an elevator, which we took to the fifth floor. This wasn't the famous MI6 building - that was a couple of blocks west along the river- but it still had the feel of a security centre: everyone had badges hanging from chains or clipped to their waistband and I'd only made it as far the entrance hall because my name and photo ID was already on a list:

Capt. Mark Barrett, it said. Army Air Corps.

Which was a stretch.

I hadn't flown in years. The army had hurled me and my DD about as far away as they could manage, which was to Battersea, and life as a courier. I enjoyed the freedom and the money wasn't too bad, but the sight of my former rank and designation still gave me a shiver.

We left the elevator and walked along a quiet, carpeted corridor until we stopped and Tom carded a door, then we entered a room, which was quieter and even more carpeted than the corridor. There was a desk, with a chair on each side, and two dark green folders sitting on top. Tom sat down on one chair and I sat down opposite him. He picked up the folders in turn, checked the contents, and then looked up to face me. 'How're you doing these days?'

'I'm good,' I said.

'Working as a courier,' he added. He paused, pacing himself. 'I bet that suits you,' he said.

I gave the smallest of smiles, it did actually. 'You still with the Regiment?'

In the British army there are many regiments, but there is only one Regiment. That is the Special Air Service. The SAS. The elite of elites. And Tom was born to it. He was, in reality, an elite killer and leader of men, and somehow, I couldn't quite figure him working admin in an MI-6-adjacent building in Vauxhall. He nodded, glanced at his civvies, reading my thoughts. 'I'm liaising with Six, and various other international security organisations: You've heard that Xao is visiting our green and pleasant land in a few weeks?'

Xao was the new Chinese Premier. More Confucian than Communist, he'd succeeded Xi and had continued the Chinese drive towards world-domination while keeping the Chinese 'world' itself intact. As far as globalism and China went, it was a one-way street: the world got globalized but China stayed firmly Chinese. In the USA, Chinese cash had bought up half the tech, most of the media and a good proportion of the sports teams, though perhaps not quite so many here in the UK, where they were in competition with the house of Saud. China had bribed or bought most of Africa into compliance, and were busy doing the same with the EU. And they'd paid for everything using the money we'd given them for the stuff they made for us, which was cheaper and more ubiquitous than the stuff from anywhere else in the world.

'State visit,' I said.

'Think of it as a Royal Procession,' he said. 'The freshly-minted Emperor surveying his lands, his people and his supplicants.'

'He's the most powerful man in the world,' I said, 'But he still dyes his hair.' Tom almost smiled at this. He pushed forward the two files still smiling, and I asked him, 'What are these?'

'These are debts being paid,' he said. 'That shitstorm back in 'Stan wasn't your fault, but you paid the price.'

'I assaulted a senior officer in a war zone.'

'That will do the trick,' he said. 'But that's not why they canned you.'

'The drugs?'

He nodded. 'The drugs,' he said.

Five years earlier I'd been with a squad of SAS troopers, my helicopter got downed and we were holed up in a remote valley very close to the Chinese border. For three days we endured a shootout with the taliban, the *students*, as the word is translated from Urdu, during which time we discovered a cache of arms, and below that, fifty kilos of uncut heroin. As senior officer, I'd authorised it all to be blown to kingdom-come, it wasn't quite Corporal Hicks saying "nuke em from orbit," but it was close, and the rescue party, which numbered an American spook amongst the GIs, were not best pleased, as it threw a spanner into their plans for opening a pipeline into which they could inject narcotics into the Chinese mainland. Much as Britain had done two hundred years earlier, and sort of like what China was doing to us, except they were giving us iPhones and news-bots in lieu of the more traditional narcotics. It was my turn to smile. 'Burning thirty million quid's worth of heroin will also do the trick,' I said.

I hadn't touched the folders, and he noticed, drawing them back to his side of the desk and tappng each with a fingertip. 'Two folders,' he said. 'Two offers. Both are good, and neither cost you anything.'

'Everything costs something,' I said.

'You've spent five years paying in advance.' He pushed forward one folder, 'This one: the brass took a look at your DD. They reversed their decision.'

'Reversed it?'

'Yes. Officially it never happened.'

He watched me, looking for a reaction. Despite the light tone, this was a hugely important thing he was throwing at me, and he wanted to see my reaction. I chose not to react. Later on, I might go for a celebratory pint, but right now I wanted more detail.

'They don't reverse decisions,' I said, finally.

'Two reasons,' Tom said. 'One. The Colonel in question was a massive cock and a complete liability. And he has gone.'

'Him being a liability doesn't excuse me breaking his nose,' I said.

'There were quite a few disciplinary cases he'd instigated. Over a couple of decades, quite a few people lost their careers due to his behavior. He was a Guards Colonel and a general cunt; he bombed out a number of decent officers and men. The brass chose a half dozen cases at random, to make right.

And you're one of them.' He could tell I wasn't convinced. The army is many things, but random? No. He leaned forward a little, resting lightly on an elbow while he scanned the contents, then continued, '"Reversal of Dishonourable Discharge into Honourable Discharge. Back payment of five years' pay, to the date of the original decision, at the rank of Captain, plus seniority and lost benefits."' He stopped reading and added, 'Plus the return of your pilot's license, should you decide you want to fly again.'

Should I want to fly *again?* I almost laughed out loud at this. I rode my motorbike too fast, too often, hoping to catch air over every bump and pothole. I dreamt I was levitating. I daydreamed of flying every time I had a free moment. *Should I want to* fly *again?* I'd strangle a nun to get back my license.

I said nothing.

Tom closed that folder.

'The other?' I asked.

This made him grin again. 'I knew you wouldn't be impressed,' he told me. 'The thing they said about you: that you don't flake out, no matter what happens. You might go a bit berserk, but you don't lose it.'

'Who are *they*?'

'Moose. Toffee. Wake.'

The SAS boys I'd fought alongside, five years ago. The toughest, chillest, most piss-taking and matter-of-fact killers I'd ever worked with. And Meakin, of course, who'd died, and he was the best of them. It was high praise. 'How's War Zone?' I asked. War Zone was the stray dog we'd found in that godforsaken valley, adopted, and which Toffee had taken back to the Regiment.

'Old and fat and very content,' he said. 'The QM up in Hereford is taking good care of him.' He opened the second folder. 'This one: rescinded DD, back pay and benefits, as per,' he said. 'But in this case, you're back in the army like you never left, fast-track to Major, and,' and at this point his smile became a little evil, 'You come work for me.'

I wasn't expecting this.

He said, 'You're an excellent pilot, Mark. Capable. Fearless. And you're well liked in the Regiment.'

'I'm not doing selection,' I said. SAS selection is one of the most horrendous processes in the world and I had no desire to put myself through that.

He shook his head. 'No selection. You join 8 Flight and we give you a civilian Dauphin to fly, updated to fuck with more toys than a container ship from China. What's not to like?'

Indeed, I thought, looking both gift horses straight in the mouth. He closed the second folder. 'It's a lot to think about. Either way you get back your rank, you get back-pay, and you can fly again. But don't give me an answer now. Take a week or two to think about it.' He pushed the folders forward. 'Have your brother check out the legal side,' he added, reading my mind. It was exactly what I was planning to do. My brother James is a barrister, his chambers just a couple of miles away, across the river. I would

definitely be running this conversation past him. I took the folders. 'Got time for a beer?' Tom asked. The official side now completed, he was suddenly friendly again. I checked my watch, half-three.
'Two beers,' I said.

Ten minutes later we stepped in through the door of The Black Dog and I went to the bar, bought us each a pint of dark, limited-edition cask ale, then followed him to a table in the corner.
'The Regiment is going to be busy over the next few years,' Tom said, after he'd taken a long draw from the glass. 'The MOD think wars can be won by a combination of intel, drones and the occasional insertion of special forces.' He frowned, 'They have an army that could comfortably fit into the Olympic Stadium to watch West Ham United on a rainy Tuesday evening. A navy that can be taken out by two or three guided missiles. An air force that will survive maybe a half-dozen hostile encounters.'
'And you'.
The Regiment, I meant.
'And us.' He took another pull at his beer. 'This is good,' he said before returning to the subject at hand. 'They think wars are too dirty. Too many body-bags. Too much collateral. And too expensive by half. Then there's the fact that no one wants to join the army in the first place. We're outnumbered by every other army on earth, our leadership is obsessed with equity and fairness, and putting women into the frontline, which' he added, 'I have no problem with,

except for the fact they're reducing the physical requirements to up the quotas. Which means we have soldiers who can march ten miles with a fifty-pound pack whereas they used to march twenty and carry a hundred-ten.' He finished his pint with a slurp, stood, and went to the bar for another round. When he came back he added, 'Scotland are desperate to leave the union, so we lose the jocks who, by the way, make great fighters, when they're not crying into their whiskey about the fucking highland glens. Which leaves us, the Marines, the Paras and the PBI.'

'You getting this all of your chest, Tom?' I teased.

He nodded, 'Too fucking right. Until you sign those papers you're a civilian, but you're still owned by the official secrets act, so you're in that grey area where I can tell you shit I couldn't tell anyone else. Besides,' he said, 'It's not all bad news. England was always better as a small, independent nation. The Empire was a mistake, the East India Company metastasized and we ended up owning half the fucking world, a role for which we were barely qualified. I doubt we'll make that schoolboy error again. I'm hoping we'll go back to doing what we do best.'

'Which is?'

'Drinking beer, taking the piss, and making a barely legal living as an international pirate state.'

'Sounds like my lifestyle,' I said.

'In-fucking-deed,' he said, as though I'd proved his point.

A half-hour later we were on our third pint, which was fine by me, today I was unemployed, though I had work booked for tomorrow. 'You mentioned Xao?' I said.

'Yeah. He's arriving soon and the security forces are shitting a brick. It's not that we think someone will kill him, though that's always a possibility, stuffing a million Uyghurs into concentration camps while attempting to impose a protection racket onto the rest of the world will put a dent in your popularity.'

'So what are they scared of?' I asked.

'Xao is not liked by the islamic world, he's hated by India, and south-east Asia is terrified of him. Since the Kiwis folded to the Chinese Dollah, the Australians are desperate trying to survive a world in which China is pre-eminent. He owns most of Africa. The Russians have no goodwill towards yet another global superpower, but setting aside the Ukraine debacle, they're pretty-much irrelevant.'

'That's a big set-aside.'

He took a long swig of the fresh pint. 'The EU is a bust, the USA is already in China's pocket, and that was before the disgraceful fucking embarrassment of their legging it out of 'Stan with their tail embedded deeply up their arse. And so, for purely ceremonial reasons, Xao is visiting England. Like a newly ordained Pope.' He paused to wipe froth from his mouth. 'And here's the thing: the higher-ups are *desperate* to please him. They're terrified something will happen to upset him and they're kow-towing like they were born with Velcro kneepads. So yes, while they're polishing the silver and brushing down the red carpet at Buck House, we're very aware that someone, somewhere, might try to kill him, and that's where the Regiment gets involved.'

'Xao is a hard target,' I said. 'Not very gettable.'

'Everyone is gettable,' he said.

I finished my drink. 'One more, I said, and went to the bar, feeling a pleasant buzz.

When I returned, Tom checked his watch. 'Work?' I asked.

'Date.'

'Lucky you.'

'Got an hour yet,' he said, and I guessed he'd be buying another drink when we finished this one.

I like airports.

I like the movement, the hustle, the permanent invitation to *flight*. I also like the anonymity, the idea that you can disappear into a crowd. Sometimes, when I need to chill a little, I'll take the tube to Heathrow, buy a magazine from WH Smith, find a café, take a seat, plug in my headphones, switch off the alerts, listen to music, and just disappear off the map. It's not just time out. It's time to myself. A couple of days after I got the offer from Tom, I was sitting at a table in a Heathrow branch of Costa waiting to meet a client. The aftermath of covid and some heavy-duty industrial action in the months that followed, meant the airport was unusually quiet. The client was late, but mild weather meant that the few people who were in the airport were dressed appropriately, and that included some very attractive women. Which is always a bonus. I wasn't complaining but I was mentally prepping myself to write-off the meeting as a bust, when a figure approached me.

'Mr. Barrett?'

He was mid-thirties, average size and build, wearing the euro-drifter outfit of jeans, trainers, a hoodie, and a lightweight backpack, and although I was wearing cotton trousers and a t-shirt, and my backpack was a cheap Chinese knock-off, not original Acr/teryx like his, we could both have been dressed by the same person. He was smiling at me, I stood, and we shook hands. 'Mr Hair?'

'Please to meet you, Mr. Barrett.'

He'd called me the evening before, asked if we could meet up. I'd suggested he pop around to my basement flat, something I wouldn't usually do but I was in the middle of putting together the engine on my 1977 Moto Guzzi 850T, and I preferred to work while I waited. He'd agreed and then, unexpectedly, he'd called me earlier and asked if we could meet here. I'd been busy blackening my knuckles in a vain attempt to tighten the nuts on the engine block, which were old, worn and reluctant, and I was glad of the chance to get out of the house for an hour.

'Good to meet your too,' I said, but as I looked at him and registered his accent, I adjusted my mental spelling of his name to *Herr*. 'Can I get you a coffee?' I added, not waiting for a reply but walking to the counter.

'An Americano would be good,' he said. I ordered us one each then went back to the table. He smiled again as I sat down, pushed a coffee towards him. 'What can I do for you?' I asked.

'I have a task for you, if you can complete it.' He said, taking a slight sip of the coffee. 'It is a package to be delivered. But I don't have the recipient's address.'

'You have a name?'

'Yes.' He took out a slip of paper and gave it to me. Zemar Ridai. Address unknown. Attached to the back of the paper with a clip was a photograph of a middle-eastern looking man with a beard. I pondered this for a moment. My history with bearded men in turbans wasn't great. I'd been to war with a bunch of them. Neither did I want to insert myself into someone else's possible stalking situation. 'You know you can get private detectives to find people?'

'I'll pay you for finding him, and for delivering the package.' He must have seen the look on my face and added hastily, 'I'm not looking to find him, so when you do locate him, you don't need to tell me. In fact, I'd like it part of our agreement that you keep this entirely to yourself. Simply gave him the envelope.'

I paused, took a drink of my coffee, as much to give me time to think as anything else, then said, 'What is it you'd like me to deliver to him.'

'A letter. Some photographs.'

My phone rang. I pressed the red button and it stopped. I said, 'Is he a friend? A client?'

'I hardly know him, and we have no business relationship,' he said. 'I'm going away for some time and this is an errand of mostly sentimental value.'

I watched two trolley-dolleys walk by, both tugging wheelie cases, both gorgeous, and both unobtainable. I took a long breath and turned back to Mr. Herr thinking that London is a big place to find a single man whose address I don't know, on behalf of a client whose motives I don't know either. He read my mind. 'I understand, you don't want to be put in an awkward situation,' he said, 'But I can assure you there is nothing illegal in what I'm asking you to do.'

'If there were any issues,' I said, 'If for example, this was laundered money, if you were a jealous ex, if anything smelled dodgy, then you know I would hand over all the information to the police.' I said this clearly and slowly on the off-chance this was a police sting, but it didn't feel like one. He came across as a genuine, if slightly-awkward customer.

He said, 'I understand. There is nothing illegal in what I'm asking you to do. I am not a wronged former business partner, nor am I a jealous ex-spouse.'

'Assuming that, then you have my complete confidence,' I said. My phone rang again. I pressed red again.

'I'll pay you for the courier service plus a finder's fee for locating him,' he said, 'And I will trust you to keep your end of the bargain. I will expect that you do not tell me any more than, you accept the job, then I will leave the details to you.'

'But what if I don't find him?'

'I'm sure you will.'

'But what,' I persisted, 'if, let's say, after a year, I haven't found him, and you return and I'm still sitting on package.'

His face turned serious, his voice a touch more earnest. 'I trust you, Mr. Barrett.'

'You don't know me, Mr. Herr.'

'Allow me to trust you nevertheless.'

He checked his watch. Took a careful sip of his coffee.

My phone rang again.

'If you haven't found him after a year,' carefully putting down the coffee mug and wiping the rim and the handle with a tissue, 'Then you can dispose of the documents. There's no intrinsic value to them.'

'Do you mind if I answer this?' I said, meaning the phone.

'Of course.'

I pressed green and held the phone to my ear.

'Barrett.'

'Hey Barrett, it's Millie.'

Millie was my upstairs neighbour. We'd swapped numbers months ago on the off-chance one of us got burgled or had a flood or something. 'What's up Mills,' I said.

'Do you know the cops are in your place?' she said. 'They just bust down the door and they're swarming all over it.'

A half-hour later, I threw some notes at the Uber driver, leapt out of his Citröen, and ran towards, and then under, the police tape surrounding the door of my flat, glancing up briefly to see Millie staring down at me from her living room window above my front door. Millie gave me a brief wave, phone in hand. I slowed as I approached the uniformed cop standing at my door. 'What's going on?' I asked.

He looked at me with an expressionless face. 'And you are?'

'I'm the owner of this flat.'

'Mark Barrett?' a voice said from behind.

I turned to see a red-faced bloke dressed in police-casual, 'Yes?' I asked, feeling more than a tad pissed-off. 'Do you want to...'

He reached into his jacket, withdrew a plastic gun.

'Tell me you're not going to...' I said, my heart sinking with the realisation of what was about to happen.

He tasered me.

Unexpectedly, I survived.
Trauma teams. Field surgery. More surgery,
Physiotherapy. Recovery. 80% then 90%, then 100%.
Eventually I became fitter than I had been before:
leaner, quicker, quieter. I called it the 7.62 Health
Plan. It removes all unnecessary extras. Especially
doubt.

Finally, I found myself back home, looking round and
wondering who I was. Wondering who my family
were. Wondering who Rhetta was. Something had
got lost in me. And all the time, the knowledge that I
had survived, and the words I had spoken when I
thought I was dying. Those words were a debt. You
pay a price for everything you do, I thought,
remembering something I'd read somewhere. And
you pay a price for everything you don't do. No one
gets to not pay a price. You get to choose your
poison, that's it.

But which poison would I choose?

For a year I drifted, searching for the debt, and for how to repay it, and while I drifted, I chose to become strong, I chose to read, and I chose to reflect. But still the debt seemed indistinct, I couldn't find it, I could not follow it. Worse, the family to whom I had returned no longer knew me, nor I them. I removed myself from their lives, from the confusion, from the pain they felt.

Then one day, sitting in a cafe, enjoying a coffee, I read an article about the drug cartels in central America. About how their work destroyed people, destroyed cities, destroyed nation states. It had nothing to do with me with me, I thought. But towards the end of the article I read the sentence: "These are men for whom consequences do not exist" and I thought, there have *to be consequences, there* has *to be a price paid. If there is no price, if we act within a moral void, then we are mere beasts. I knew this was not true. Men could be noble. They could sacrifice. I had seen it demonstrated. I had seen a man had risk his life to save me, and risk it again to save the life of a mortal enemy.*

And there was my debt, I realised. The knowledge that men were not beasts. The knowing that debts must be paid. But how to pay mine? How to pay the price of the words I had spoken and repay the world on behalf of the man who had saved me? I had few skills, and small experience of life beyond the rifle and the pack.

I gave it further thought.

'Mark!' a female voice said.

'Ruby?' I asked, taking a second or two to recognise her voice on the other end of the phone. Ruby is a Colonel in military intelligence. She's on the rise and I don't doubt she'll be a general in a few years. She was also the second military type I'd spoken to in as many weeks. Before that, I was lucky if I spoke to them on an annual basis. I was curious, to say the least.

'How are you getting on?' she asked. I could hear office noises in the background.

'I'm good,' I said.

'Are you busy?' she asked.

'Not at this moment.'

'Come over to Whitehall. I'll buy you lunch.'

'When?'

'An hour?' she said.

'See you then.'

I put down the phone. Who can refuse a lunch date with a beautiful woman in a restaurant situated in the heart of military power for the United Kingdom of Great Britain and Northern Ireland?

Not me.

An hour later I was standing on Whitehall.

Ruby, as per, was on time, climbing out of a taxi exactly sixty minutes after our call, sweeping me in through a portico where she signed the book, and then walking us confidently through the building to the rear, where there was a garden table waiting for us. She sat down facing the building, which meant my back was to the doors, but I figured, being in the bowels of Whitehall I was pretty safe.

'Hungry?'

She knew the way to a man's heart.

We ordered food, and Ruby ordered us both a beer while we waited. When the waiter returned with the drinks we each took a long gulp and enjoyed the occasion. Ruby was one of those girls who would make a great wife or a great friend, either would have been fine with me, though the wife thing was probably out of the question, her career wouldn't thrive on marrying an ex-Captain with a questionable service history.

'So,' I said.

She nodded. 'So.' She glanced at me, almost coy. 'Do you want the official version or the patented Ruby version.'

'Give me yours. I have a jaundiced view of officials.'

'I can imagine.' She took another long sup, let out a satisfied sigh and put down her glass. 'Right. Officially, I have some colleagues who are shitting a brick that you're going to sue them. Or worse, sell your story to the Daily Mail.'

'What for?'

'That *debacle* of an arrest last week. It wouldn't have been quite so bad for us, but your helpful neighbour recorded the entire thing on her phone, and uploaded it live to Periscope.'

'I'm not planning on suing anyone,' I said. 'Or calling the Mail.'

'They took you to the station and questioned you.'

'I was barely conscious.'

'I've seen the video tape. It was a complete shitshow.' She did not look pleased.

'Did you know they were going to raid my place?'

'I didn't connect the dots until later, it was just a flat in Battersea.'

'What were they looking for?'

'You don't know?'

I shook my head, thinking, why were military intelligence involved in an abortive police raid on my flat? The food arrived, and this gave Ruby time to prepare an answer that would satisfy me, in the sense of me not suing the police or Special Branch or any other arm of national security, without giving away anything that she didn't have to. I didn't realise this until later, of course, and besides, the food was good. The beer too. So we ate. And drank.

Eventually she wiped her mouth on a napkin and said, 'We're on the hunt for a person of interest. He was in contact with you, though at the time we had little more than an address, so we didn't know it was you, just some anonymous bloke at an address.'

'A quick peek on the electoral register would have told you,' I said, pausing to take another go at the beer, which had been mysteriously topped up while I wasn't looking, with a freshly opened bottle standing beside the glass.

'Don't I fucking know it.'

'Do you need any information from me?' I asked.

She paused to look me in the eye. 'No.'

'Who was it you're interested in?'

'If you don't know, then I can't tell you.'

Which left me in the dark, because I didn't know.

'Food's good,' I said.

An hour later we were leaving the restaurant, the meal paid for by the state, as a sort of apology for smashing up my gaff and giving me a mild concussion when my head hit a brick wall after I was tasered. Ruby assured me that if they needed any more information, they'd knock. And ask nicely. I still didn't know who they were looking for. I deal with a lot of shady characters. Most people send their packages by Royal Mail, or MyHermes. The sort of people who use couriers tend to be a small group, self-selected for less-than-scrupulous activities. The idea that one of those customers had got himself in bad graces was not surprising. I decided to walk off the beer and the food and took the route along the embankment, over Vauxhall Bridge, and along the south bank of the river, past the power station. On a good day this'd take me not much more than an hour, but today, with a warm sun, a belly full of food and alcohol, and a semi-formal apology from Ruby on behalf of god-knows-who, it took a bit longer.

Still, by the time I got home, I was pretty much sober.

The new door, recently fitted to replace the smashed-in one, was stiff on the hinges, the lock shiny and new, the thick brass key feeling heavy and strange in my hand. I'd paid a lot of money for this new door. It wasn't exactly *armoured*, but it was seriously heavy-duty. Ruby said there'd be a cheque landing in my bank account to cover 'all expenses', after which it would be assumed by all parties that the entire affair was closed. Fair enough, I have a thick head. And now I had a new door. The fact they'd taken my phone and my laptop was irritating, but everything was backed up, Greener was going to send me some new kit, and compensation was heading my way. I locked the door behind me, and fell asleep on the sofa. It was close to five that afternoon when I was woken by a rap on the window.

I opened the door to see a shifty-looking kid carrying a box. 'Delivery for Mark Barrett?' he asked.

'I dunno. Is it?' I replied.

He handed me the box. 'Laptop and phone. Greener said to tell you, you should think about using a tablet...' he looked faintly embarrassed, whether it was passing on the message or the fact I used a laptop, he didn't say.

'Thanks,' I said.

'Also,' he said, taking a gizmoid from his shoulder bag, 'He said I need to do a sweep.'

'A sweep?' I asked, as he stepped past me and into my flat, raising his index finger to his lips. I watched as he switched on the little box and began to sector my room, walking back and forwards, until, as he approached one wall, a light in his electronic box began to flash, He paused, held it close to a light switch, and it began to flash so quickly the flashing light merged into one single beam. He took a post-it note from a pocket and stuck it to the light switch. Finished in this room, he went into the kitchen and repeated the process, affixing post-it notes to another light switch. Then he went into my bedroom,

I followed, and he worked his way around, sticking a post-it to my bedside lamp, and then, pausing for a sliver of a moment, another to the frame of my bed. I left him to do the bathroom, sitting back down in my sofa, then I heard him in the basement. After ten minutes he came back into the living room, motioned for me to follow him and we stepped out into the street.

Standing below the streetlamp, he switched off his little machine. 'Bugs,' he said, looking up. 'I found six, including a sneaky one in the wiring of your motorbike. Nice machine by the way. Classic.'

'Thanks,' I said. 'Bugs?'

'Listening devices. A tracker on your bike.' He slid the bug-hunter back into his bag, 'No cameras I could find but lots of little ears to hear what you're saying. There might be some I've missed, but Shady doesn't usually miss much. I just updated her a couple of days ago.'

'Shady?'

He patted the electronic box that was now snug inside his bag.

'Greener asked you to do this?'

He nodded, as though it was obvious. 'He said I should deliver the gear, then do a search for bugs, mark them, but not destroy them.'

'So I know they're listening.'

'But they don't *know* you know. So, you can make it work for you.'

'Right,' I said.

'Disinformation,' he said. 'It's the thing.'

'Well, thank you,' I said.

He gave me a card. 'Any probs, or if you want me to remove them, give me a call. Oh, and I should tell you, four of those bugs were UK Government-issue.'

I frowned in confusion.

'Two of them weren't,' he clarified.

'What're you telling me?'

He shrugged. 'There's more than one player in this game.'

'You're taking the piss, right?'

'Shady never lies.' He patted his bag again. 'All the bugs are fresh, new batteries. They've been put in within the last couple of days.' I rubbed my eyes, my memories of the afternoon spent with Ruby had taken on a sinister sheen. Someone had bugged my flat. Then someone else had done the same. 'You been meeting new people recently?' he asked, his voice the tone of a kindly doctor enquiring as to the source of an embarrassing STD. 'You might have alarmed someone.'

'I'm beginning to think I have.'

'You know who you've upset?'

'No.'

'Ignorance is no defence,' he said, slightly ominously, then, 'I have to go.' He looked over the road and a blacked-out 5 Series switched on its lights, the engine purring as it rolled across to where we stood. 'Keep in touch if you need anything.'

'Thanks,' I said.

'No probs.' He raised a fist in salute and I bumped it with mine.

Fight the power.

'Don't let them Josef K you,' he said as he walked away, then climbed into the passenger seat of the Beemer, which closed behind him. I watched the car drive away into the evening.

There's a Costa at Clapham Junction, just round the corner from me, and it was open so I went in and bought a large coffee, sat at a table and took out the laptop and phone from the box that Greener had sent me. The phone was generic smartphone with, no doubt, some extra bits and pieces added. Greener had a whole cottage industry based around supercharging and masking IT equipment. I switched it on, checked the number, which was new to me, reminding myself to update my details with the appropriate people. Then I took out the laptop and nearly laughed. It was about two inches thick. Made of extremely roadworn black plastic, and when I opened the lid I saw it came equipped with a trackball. I laughed quietly, picked up the phone on which, under JG, a number was already listed and texted him. *A* Trackball!!! Then I switched it on and it booted up.

I looked up as a gaggle of Chinese students walked towards the counter, and looked back as the OS revealed that the insides were essentially a Mac. The latest operating system too. Only the outsides were from the early 1990s. I logged onto the Costa free wifi and checked my emails, found nothing new, no business, no messages from a girl, any girl, expressing her undying affection, nothing from my family, which was disappointing but also quite a relief, I wasn't in the mood for round robins about my brother Matt's kids or pictures of my brother James and his fire-breathing wife attending some society function. I used my business account to email my current clients with my latest number. Then I let out a long, slow breath, and tried to find my bearings. I had the strangest feeling that things were going sideways. There was evidence to that effect: the raid, the bugs, the sudden interest of the security forces. It hadn't gone unnoticed that I'd been contacted out of the blue by both Ruby and Tom Jarvis within a week of each other - the offer from the MOD seemed too good to be true - but I couldn't work out where the bad energy was coming from. I was reminded of the supposed quote from F Scott Fitzgerald when questioned about how his life had gone wrong, and he had replied, 'Very slowly, then all of a sudden.' I was still in the slow bit, but it felt like the all of a sudden part could happen at any moment. I took out the card that Greener's techy had given me. It simply read: Wookie. Tech Support. Followed by a telephone number. I thought of his parting words, *Don't let them Josef K you*. Indeed. But the problem with that analogy was that Josef K never knew the charges against him, so in that sense, they were *already* Josef K-ing me. I flipped off the lid on my coffee and downed half the contents. Afternoon drinking invariably left me feeling sleepy,

Ruby and me had put away a fair few drinks along with the food, so despite the nap I'd taken earlier, I knew I'd sleep tonight. In the meantime, the almost-hot coffee worked its caffeine magic as it spread through the blood vessels and capillaries of my consciousness, and I began to wake properly as I went through my emails, and part of that awakening was the gradual realisation of what had happened in my home while I was out. Realisation was swiftly replaced by anger. Some fucker was fucking with my fucking home, for reasons I did not fucking know. I was becoming seriously pissed off. The offer from the Ministry began to annoy me almost as much as being tasered by the cop, it was all of a piece, I realised, though I didn't know how it was all connected. I picked up Wookie's card and texted him. *What's the worst sound you can make into those hidden microphones?*

He texted back almost immediately. *I could put a high-pitched, high-decibel whine down their throat. He added, Imagine standing next to a jet engine on full power.*

I texted back, *Can you make it happen to all the bugs at the same time?*

He replied. *With pleasure.*

I texted back. *Can you be back at mine, tomorrow morning, about nine?*

He texted me back a thumbs-up.

That'll do for a start, I thought.

Fortified by coffee and anger, using my new/old laptop and the Costa wifi, I searched online for 'extreme porn sound-effects' and downloaded an MP3 file. When I got home I loaded this sound file onto an old iPod I had left in the basement for when I was working on the bike. Then I plugged the iPod into my sound system, set it to repeat, and pressed *play*. Accompanied by the sound of over-stressed bouncing bed-springs, panting, groans, seventies disco music, and what might have been a squealing pig, I popped in some soft earplugs, set my phone alarm to vibrate, took off my clothes and climbed into bed. I woke eight hours later to the vibrations of the alarm and otherwise silence.

The iPod battery had run flat.

About 6.30 the next morning, I went for a run. Running isn't something I do a lot of. Living in London you can stay fit just walking from place to place, but I needed a blast of fresh air, so I pulled on a t-shirt and shorts, laced up my battered trainers and took to the street. I don't usually go for long distances - short and fast is my preferred mode of running - but this morning, after about ten minutes, I found myself approaching the Albert Bridge and getting my second wind, so instead of turning back, I took a right into Battersea Park, following the river as far as Chelsea Bridge, then turning right until I got to the boating lake, following the path in a rough circle as I ran beneath the avenues of trees, the gorgeous houses of Prince of Wales Drive on my left, then past the astro-turf pitches until I got back to the Prince Albert Bridge. The day was mild and the sun was shining, and I had a residue of anger to burn off, so I did the entire circuit again. When I was almost home, I checked my watch, I'd been out for about forty minutes, and I slowed down to a walk, sweating and hot, my heart and lungs working like industrial bellows. I spotted Wookie waiting patiently outside my house. I checked my watch again. It was barely seven. 'I thought we agreed to meet up at nine,' I said.

'Spooks don't start work at nine,' he said. 'Early bird and all that.'

I didn't bother to mention that anyone bugging my place would be using a recording device. They wouldn't need to be up early. He followed me in, and was followed by two other guys, who set down their equipment. My squad,' he said.

'Have at it,' I said, and went for a shower.

An hour later, I was showered, shaved and dressed, and Wookie's squad were finishing up. Again we went outside to talk, and he said, 'We've isolated the microphones and inserted a connection that means all they hear is a high-pitched scream. You won't hear it, it's purely an electronic signal.'

'Great, so I can forget about them?'

'Probably better to have them removed after a couple of days. You can sell 'em on eBay.'

'You can have them,' I said, 'If they're any use.'

'I can always use bugging devices.' He paused, 'Oh, and we found a camera too. I missed it first time round. It was hidden behind the glass control panel of your oven. My machine missed it cos it was stashed deep inside the electronics.'

'A camera.'

Wookie gave me a slow smile. 'Unless you get up to nonsense in the kitchen, it shouldn't be too bad.' I shrugged, feeling the anger building again. I hadn't got up to *nonsense* in the kitchen in months but it'd be nice to be able to do so without someone snooping via a hidden camera. Wookie said, 'We isolated that too, and looped a strobe signal, calibrated to induce epilepsy. Anyone watching it will get a headache, a seizure, or the shits, depending on their constitution.'

Wookie had way with words.

His squad packed up and left; Wookie looked around, then said. 'This is on Greener so no charge, but I'll have the bugs and camera if you don't want 'em.'

'Come back in a couple of days,' I said. 'Take them.'

'I will. I'll do another sweep while I'm at it. Oh, some other things. I bugged your laptop. It will record anyone who uses it. And I've put a micro camera up there, movement triggered.' He pointed to the corner of the living room. 'There's a hyperlink on this card where you can go to see a playback of events. And don't use your wifi. They can legally authorise downloads of your online activities.' I didn't ask who *they* were. 'I'll sort you out a VPN,' he added, and left. I went back inside to make myself some breakfast. The run had triggered my hunger. I glanced at the oven when I went into the kitchen, thinking, *traitor*.

Suddenly very suspicious of my surroundings, I decided against opening my emails at home, which was beginning to feel alien, and just a little bit threatening. I still didn't know why the police had raided me or who they were looking for. Nor was I sure who had bugged the place in my absence.

Wookie had uncovered bugs, but there might be more. He might have missed some. *They* might have visited while I was out and installed some more. My home was beginning to feel like when a girl you're seeing suddenly changes her profile to private and keeps stepping outside to take calls from 'work'. Sighing, I slid the laptop into my rucksack, hefted it onto my shoulder, and left my flat. I turned right at the gate and headed on foot towards cheap coffee and free wifi.

Costa has slightly better coffee, but it was busy, and when I looked in through the windows I saw that MaccyDs was unaccountably quiet, so I went in there, ordered a large black coffee and a blueberry muffin, found a seat and got settled. I unslung my laptop, powered up, and opened my emails to see if there was anything that required immediate attention. Nothing. But there was a nice surprise waiting in my bank account, so that was fine. I glanced at the two envelopes that Jarvis had given me still sitting in my rucksack. I had a decision to make, but I'd yet to give it much thought. I took a writing pad and pencil from of the rucksack and drew a line down the middle of the page, wrote *pros* on one side and *cons* on the other. I couldn't think of many pros. I was five years out, my mindset had changed, my approach to life, which had always been slightly to the cavalier side, had gone so far in that direction now, that I knew I couldn't handle the rules and regulations of being in the army again.

Or could I?

Under *cons* I wrote: I like being my own boss.

It worked for me. From being a tiny cog in a huge machine, I was now the only cog in a one-cog machine. I went back to *pros*, thought for a long moment, then wrote: I won't have to think.

It wasn't much of a pro but it was true: in the army you follow orders. Within that, on a moment to moment basis, you can think for yourself, but you really don't have to. As a pilot I was rarely in charge of the mission. I simply picked people up at point A and dropped them at point B. If we took fire I took evasive action. If the door gunner began cursing me out I knew I should take *more* evasive action. But flying wasn't thinking. I wouldn't have to think at all. I could spend fifteen years flying, not thinking too much, and enjoying a hell of a lifestyle. But still, I couldn't imagine going back. Civvy street had spoiled me. I didn't think I could ever bend my will to some braying Colonel or accept suicidal orders with a grin and a can-do attitude as I'd done in the past. Which left the other option: accept the Honourable Discharge and take the five years Captain's pay, which was what Tom said I was due. The prospect of which should have been lovely, probably close to two hundred thousand, after the Inland Revenue took their no-doubt large slice off the top. I could take a year off, travel...I immediately discarded this idea. It didn't feel right.

I hadn't *been* a Captain for those five years. I hadn't been in combat. I hadn't been risking my life or shouldering responsibility, as a Captain no-doubt would, so taking the money felt wrong. It felt hollow. I checked the email address on the paperwork and began typing:

Hi Tom, my decision re the generous choice relayed by you:
I do appreciate it, it's not often you get a do-over, but I don't want either option. It's five years too late for the first, I've moved on and I can't go back. And I didn't earn the second - I know what earning five years' pay costs a soldier, so I can't take it.
I'll keep my DD.
The army can keep the cash.

I hesitated for only a millisecond, then pressed send. I sat back, feeling slightly sick for turning down so much money, idly spinning the trackball on my battered, ancient laptop with the outward look of a 1994 Compaq and the innards of a state-of-the-art MacBook.
I heard a giggle.
I looked up to see a girl who looked very much like a grown-up version of Mulan looking at my laptop. She smiled at me, a mix of openness and some slight calculation in her expression. 'Trackball,' she said, pointing out the obvious.
'Yes,' I said.
'Do you like old-tech?' she asked. She really was cute. Heavy fringe, perfect cheekbones, eyes the colour of tree-bark.

'I got this from a friend when I lost my old machine,' I said. 'I think he meant it as a bit of a joke.'

'I like it,' she said, leaving a pause that can only be described as pregnant, and into which, to fill the space, I happily leapt. 'Would you like to try it?'

She pushed her hair behind an ear, nodded, and for a moment I thought she hadn't understood, but then she picked up her bag and coffee and came over to my table and sat down facing me. I pushed it over for her to look, and she turned the screen a little to face her. She pressed a key, rolled the trackball under an index finger, smiling broadly. 'What operating system?' she asked.

It's a mac underneath,' I told her.

'Can I go online?' she asked.

'Sure.'

I wondered briefly if she was about to download some barnyard-porn, but checked myself, that sort of thing only happened amongst close male friends. I watched as she opened google, did a search for Greenwich Uni, saw her dial in a specific department, then she found photographs of a class, mostly other Chinese students, and I saw that she was in the photos. She smiled to herself, took out her phone and took a snapshot of the laptop. then closed down the search and pushed the laptop back to me.

'I'm Mark,' I told her.

'May,' she replied, doing her hair-behind-the-ears thing.

'Can I buy you a coffee?' I asked.

'I have a class in an hour,' she said, pulling a sad face. 'I have to go soon.' She began organising the books she'd carried over to my table.

'I'm done here too,' I said, finishing my coffee. 'Can I walk out with you?'

'Ok,' she said, packing all her gear into a huge shoulder bag. 'Do you live in Clapham?' she asked, standing and hoisting the bag, which looked like it weighed as much as she did, though she couldn't have weighed much more than ninety pounds fully clothed. She was wearing pink converse and faded jeans, along with a Joe Strummer sweatshirt, and I was suddenly very aware of the at least ten-year age gap between us.

'Battersea, just along the road a bit,' I said, as we walked to the door and stepped out onto St. John's Road. We turned left towards the Clapham Station, walking in silence for a few moments and I thought, perhaps she was just being polite. I decided to leave her at the corner with a friendly but courteous smile, when she suddenly said, 'I could meet you after my lecture?'

'Ok,' I said. Things were brightening up. 'What time do you finish?'

'Six.'

I pointed at the pub over the road, The Falcon. 'Let's meet in there.'

'Sure,' she said. 'I can be here for seven.'

'Great. Seven.'

'See you then,' she said, pushing her hair back, and I let her turn right towards the tube station while I waited at the corner for moment, wondering what I should do for the next three hours. She crossed the road, turned and gave me a wave, then disappeared amongst the mid-afternoon pedestrians.

A minute before seven, showered, shaved and gleaming, I pushed in through the double doors of the Falcon, found the place fairly quiet, and went to the bar to order a pint. As I stood waiting, a felt a presence by my side and turned to see May, who appeared even more tiny than my brief acquaintance had suggested. She smiled, 'Hi.'

'What would you like to drink?' I asked.

'White wine, please.'

She had that charming way of speaking English but missing out random articles and consonants. But, I reflected, she spoke way better English than I did Mandarin. I ordered a wine then turned to her. 'How was college.'

She pulled a face. 'Boring.'

'What are you studying?' I asked.

'Masters in business studies,' she said.

The barman delivered the drinks and I paid with cash. I'm old-fashioned like that, both the paying, and using cash. We went to an alcove table and sat down. I raised my glass and said, 'Cheers,' and she giggled and did the same. She'd changed clothing, I don't know where or how, as she'd been to a lecture in between, but now she was wearing pink Doc Martens, a pinafore dress and a white t-shirt, over which she wore a huge cardigan. I said, 'You look lovely.'

She blushed a little and said, 'And you look very handsome.'

After three drinks and lots of chat, I asked her if she was hungry, and suggested we could go somewhere to eat, or go back to mine and order in some food. 'Do you live close?' she asked as we left the pub. I told her it was a ten-minute walk, though, as she linked her arm into mine and sort of leaned against me as we walked, it took closer to twenty. We arrived at the gate to the steps down to my basement flat, and as I unlatched it, I heard someone shout from above.

It was Millie.

'Hey,' she said, leaning out of the window, 'I have a package for you.' She disappeared back inside and then reappeared holding out a brown-paper wrapped package about the size of a paperback book. 'Catch!' she said, and dropped it into my outstretched hands.

'Thanks!' I said.'

'Have a good night,' she said, a smile teasing at the edges of her voice. I glanced at May, who was staring blank-eyed at her. She turned to me and smiled, said 'This reminds me of home' as we walked down the steps to my front door.

'How so?' I asked, struggling to unlock my new door.

'People living in 'partments, passing on messages and mail.'

'You're from Shanghai?' I said. She'd told me earlier that she'd lived there before coming to London.

'Originally my family were from Chengdu in the west of China. We moved to Shanghai when the trouble began with the Uighurs.'

I nodded, we went inside and I closed the door behind me hoping the place smelled ok. One time, my sister-in-law Adelie came to visit me, and she'd immediately opened the windows and sprayed every room with air-freshener. I'd said nothing, but took the hint, and since then I'd made an effort to keep the place fresh, but it'd been a while since I'd entertained. I watched May look around. The place didn't look too bad. Neat. Tidy. Clean. I'm an ex-soldier so cleaning and keeping tidy is automatic. 'I'll show you the place,' I said and took her to the kitchen, a brief glimpse of my bedroom, a point at the bathroom, and then the back yard from the back door. 'And downstairs is the basement,' I said.

'What's in the basement?'

'Junk,' I said, 'And my old motorbike.'

She wrinkled her nose. Not a motorbike girl, I thought.

'Can I use your bathroom,' she asked.

'Sure,' I said, and went back into the living room, opened Spotify on my laptop and chose my favourite lo-fi jazz playlist. Smiled to myself as I heard the opening bars of Ylang Ylang from KFJ. A few moments later, May came into the living room. She looked lovely. Skin like caramel milk, blue-black hair, her eyes wide and brown, her cheekbones...well, you get the idea. She walked up to me, very close, maintaining eye contact, save for a couple of times when she looked down, momentarily shy, and just waited. So I kissed her. And as our lips met, I heard the music change, almost felt the notes from a sax as they floated across the room, I could almost taste the music, and I recognised it as a track from Nubya Garcia called Together Is A Beautiful Place To Be. Too right, I thought.

The following morning, I woke late. May was gone, leaving only a parchment-coloured business card on the bedside table, on which she'd drawn a smiley face. With a groan I dragged myself out of bed and went to put on the coffee so it'd be ready when I got out of the shower. Thirty minutes later I was sitting at my kitchen table, sipping from a large mug and feeling somewhat more awake. I checked my phone and there were no messages. I opened my laptop and checked my emails. There was a reply from Tom Jarvis.

Thanks for getting back to me, Mark. Ruby predicted you'd turn it all down. Something to do with you being a knight-errant, as I recall. Says you're a modern-day Galahad, just looking for a grail. I owe her a tenner. I'll let the relevant people know. They won't be pleased, but then, I've never known you act in order to please the authorities. If you change your mind, or if you need anything, let me know. And keep in touch,
Tom.

He'd attached a photo of War Zone, the dog we'd adopted back in Arse-Cracky-Stan and who now lived with the RQM up in Hereford. He had a grey muzzle, he was a lot heavier, and he looked very happy. Small victories, I thought. I took another sip of my coffee, read the daily newspapers. Mooched about. I was on my second coffee before I looked at May's card. I'd message her later. I did want to see her again, but getting in touch too quickly might scare her off.

The rest of the day was free so I took advantage of that fact and packed my kitbag, left the flat and walked to the gym on Petworth Street. I needed a workout, hadn't stretched myself in a while. When I got there I was in luck, because Tommy Farnley was at the gym. Tommy's an ex-amateur lightweight champ whose career was derailed for a few years due to his being a criminal and having to spend an extended period of time care of HMP. He'd since pulled himself together, left behind his life of robbing armoured vans at gunpoint, and made a decent living as a boxing and fitness coach. I stripped down to shorts and a singlet, and approached him. 'You free, Tom'

'Got a cancellation. Fancy a pad session?' I nodded, and he pointed at the bags, 'Do a ten-minute warm-up then give me a shout.'

I went to wrap up my hands, pulled on my old Reyes bag mitts and stepped up to the floor-to-ceiling ball, spending five minutes getting my blood flowing, then turned my attention to a heavy bag. Tommy appeared and watched me for a few minutes. Then he said, 'Ready?'

'Sure.'

'Gumshield,' he said, and waited as I used clumsy gloved hands to pop in my gumshield. Tommy likes to hit back a bit when he's doing padwork, especially if he sees you dropping your guard. All set, I stepped into the open area with Tom, and began to hit the pads under his instructions, light and fast, like he always said: speed and accuracy, and the power will follow, go straight for the power and you'll always be too slow. Every now and again, he'd tell me, 'Guard! Keep your left up when you throw your right,' or variations. I was always dropping my left, whether it was after a jab, before a hook, or after a straight right, and Tom would tell me two or three times, then just clout me with his pad if I didn't follow instructions. After a while he nodded, satisfied, and the power began to arrive of its own accord, until I began to feel happy with the smack of glove on pad and after that I forgot myself, it was all about breathing, moving, slipping, and striking. People talk about meditation, but I think there's nothing better for clearing the mind than hitting something, and hitting it really hard, and really fast, for longer than you really want to. The gym was almost empty so we could move around a bit and the padwork became a sort of dance where I was never sure what my partner was going to do. He stopped giving me instructions and began to just raise a pad and keep it there for no more than a second or so, and I had to think on my feet and hit it. The session ended with him showing me some in-fighting techniques, including using the elbow in a clinch. Illegal in boxing, but then Tommy wasn't training me for the Queensberry rules. We finished with some pad work using my elbows from guard, then my lead elbow from no guard, a sneaky shot that travels about six inches and can knock someone unconscious with ease. Tommy called it the Kebab Shop KO. The sort of shot you'd use to remove someone from planet-consciousness for a while, if you had a row in a takeaway. Finished, I went to take a shower, and when I returned I paid him, in cash. 'Good,' he said. 'Sloppy but good. If you get in close, use that elbow, it's your best shot, you don't telegraph it. And,' he tapped his forehead, 'None of this. You'll get CTE.' Tommy knew my predilection for the headbutt in a fracas, not that I was intending to get into any fights in future. Approaching my mid-thirties, I was hoping that stuff was all behind me. He patted me on the shoulder, 'Keep your left up,' and went to find his next customer.

It was only when I got home that I remembered the package that Millie had dropped down to me the night before. I'd been preoccupied but now I saw it on the shelf in the hall where I'd left it. I poured the last of the coffee into a mug and put it into the microwave to heat it up, throwing my kit into the washbag while I waited, then took the coffee and the package to the table, drank one, looked at the other. There was a name written on the front of the envelope, Zemar Ridai. I opened google and did a quick search. There were a few people with the names Ridai and Zemar, but no one had both, and even with one name, google only had about five articles, including one giving advice on how to use dating apps to get laid. I looked at the small photograph fastened to the packet with an elastic band and I switched to google image to see if the correct Zemar Ridai appeared. Nothing. Google literally did not have a single photograph of anyone on planet earth with that name. Zemar Ridai didn't exist on the internet: I didn't know that was even possible. Having hit a blank with google, I did the next best thing and messaged Greener to ask him if he knew anyone who could so a search for someone on the QT. He got back: Sure. Send me the details. I decided to take the contract. At worst I wouldn't find him and Mr. Herr, the client, would return in a year and take back his information. Or I might find him. Either way, I'd keep a record of my search, I decided, and opened an excel document on my computer, gave it a name and entered today's date, made a note of my messages to Greener. Then I sent him the name, what details I'd been given, and copy of the photograph.

For a few days it was quiet. I had no work, and for some reason I couldn't bring myself to call May, so I passed the time working on my bike, then working out at the gym, then doing nothing and enjoying it very much. The military teaches you to be organised, but also to enjoy down-time whenever it occurs. I spent an afternoon in Battersea Park, and on another day, I passed a pleasant two or three hours looking at my favourite house in London. Well, not staring at it, but enjoying being in its presence, and watching the world go by from a riverside bench. After that I strolled to Chelsea Physic Garden and enjoyed a cup of tea as the occasional red-coated Pensioner or elderly lady in lilac and pearls meandered about. After the third consecutive day in the gym, Tommy told me to fuck off for the rest of the week and get some rest, said I wasn't a kid anymore and needed time to recover, that I'd feel it tomorrow. Tomorrow arrived and I felt fine, decided I'd spend an afternoon in Trafalgar Square and watch pretty girls, but by the time I'd walked to the Clapham tube I was beginning to feel aches in my connective tissue. By the time the tube dropped me at Charing Cross, my arms were feeling heavy. When I sat on the wall by the lions in Trafalgar Square, the aches had joined together and were having a fracas amongst themselves: my arms, legs, torso, neck and shoulders all fighting to see who could cause me the most physical discomfort.

Tommy was right, beasting myself on a daily basis was perhaps a thing of the past. Pacing myself was the future. 'Old man strength is what you're aiming for,' he'd told me.

'I'm thirty-three,' I said.

'Middle-aged,' Tommy said with a tone of definitive judgement. And sitting in the sun in the middle of London, no matter how many pretty girls and elegant women walked past, my body was agreeing wholeheartedly with Tommy. Reluctantly, I took a taxi home. I couldn't bear the tube journey or the walk. I got out at Zed's corner shop, bought a cheap bottle of wine, and went home, drank the wine, ate four brufen, read a cheap novel, and went to bed around eight. I slept deeply and woke about seven the next morning, a full eleven hours. I felt a lot better. I'd had a vague idea to sleep until 'til mid-morning, so the seven o' clock wake-up was more down to Wookie knocking on my door than me being wide awake and sharp and ready to take on the world. I opened the door and he was there, by himself, carrying a heavy bag of, no doubt, hi-tech gear. 'Morning,' I said.

'I've come for the bugs.'

'Come in,' I said, yawning. 'help yourself. I'm going back to bed.'

He nodded.

'Lock the door on your way out,' I added.

'Will do,' he said and then I was back in my pit, sleeping away the fatigue of training.

I woke around half-ten, feeling something soft and warm climbing beneath my quilt, felt their arms wrap around me. I turned, bleary-eyed, and saw May, nose to nose with me, her eyes huge at that distance.

'Wookie let me in,' she whispered. 'Go back to sleep. Wake me later,' she kissed me softly, pushing me back over again.

So I did.

By mid-afternoon, I have to admit, I was seriously hungry, so I suggested we go for something to eat. She told me she preferred to stay in bed with me so I said I'd pop out for a takeaway. She agreed, and I dressed hurriedly in t-shirt, trackie pants, and trainers, no socks, left her in my bed, half-jogged down the street meaning to grab a takeout from Piatta, a tiny bistro whose owner I knew. Fifty yards before I got there I decided to pop into the Latchmere for a quick pint. I needed the carbs, I told myself, and found myself at the bar, ordering the pasta online, and drinking beer while I waited ten minutes 'til it was ready to collect.

The pub was fairly quiet, just the barman, a couple sitting in the corner, and me. I turned as a biker came in through the door still wearing his helmet, the chin-guard folded back over the visor, and turned back to my pint, figured I had about eight minutes before the pasta was ready, and was debating whether or not I had time for a second pint.

'Mark Barrett?'

I turned. It was my client from Heathrow. 'Mr. Herr. How are you?'

'I'm very good,' he said, smiling. 'I was going to come and see you but I saw you come into the pub.'
'Great,' I said, and I meant it. I could now have the second pint, truthfully tell May I'd bumped into a client, and still be in bed, with pasta, and May, in a half hour. 'I've begun work on finding that client, 'I added.
'I have complete faith in you,' he said, 'You're a good man, Mark Barrett,' which came across a bit weird. Then he said nothing more, which was also weird. 'Would you like a drink?' I asked.
'Yes,' he said, glancing around. 'But I must go to the bathroom first.' He looked at my pint, 'I'll have whatever you're having.'
I turned to the barman and order two more pints. And I waited.
But he did not return. Puzzled, I decided to go and look. He wasn't in the toilets. I went back to the bar, finished off my pint. I thought about drinking his too when I saw flashing blue lights outside and, together with the barman, we went to the window to see armed cops dashing into a doorway. It took me a couple of moments to realise they were dashing into the doorway of the Latchmere, when they burst through the doors into the bar and pointed their guns at me, screaming something unintelligible from behind their ballistic helmets. I raised my hands, slowly. So did the barman. And the couple in the corner. Two plain clothes officer dashed in behind the stormtroopers, one of whom I recognised with a

sinking feeling. The red-face cop who'd tasered me previously.

'Don't do it,' I said.

He smiled.

Then he tasered me.

Fire and water.
From cold northern sea, a lonely road to this sun-baked desert. The route of my life has taken a turn that the Norns *did not deign to explain to me. In a foreign land they whispered their truth, and I survived, the Valkyries paused in their flight. And now I am here, waiting.*
I check my phone. The drone tells me I have four minutes. The mines are planted. The stinger uncurled. My rifle is snug against my shoulder. Calibrated. Patient, I lie in wait.

I am the heir of the shield wall and the glittering spear.
I am the price to be paid.

'I believe that's why I had to spring you out of chokey,' James told me.

Two day earlier, after the cops arrived in the pub and tasered me, I'd been cuffed, had my rights read, or so they assured me, I couldn't remember as I was in a post-ECT daze at the time, and then they dragged my arse to a cell somewhere close to Marble Arch. After repeatedly saying 'I want my lawyer, I want my lawyer, I want...' they'd allowed me to call James, a top-flight barrister who, fortuitously, is also my brother. He'd arrived, threatened to sue the everyone involved, personally, the entire thing having been captured on the pub's CCTV, and sprung me free. By the time he'd got me home, May was frantic with worry, and my still-zombified state on arrival hadn't made her mood any less close-to-hysterical. I'd gone for an early afternoon takeaway, and arrived home ten hours later, still sedated via 50,000 volts from a Special Branch taser, bruised from falling over and hitting my face on a bar stool, and generally looking like shit. James had spent some time reassuring May that I was alright, and then making sure I was, before he left me in her tender care. I didn't really come out of my brain-fog until mid-morning the following day. To be honest, days later and I still felt a bit woozy.

James had spoken directly with the Chief Constable, and sent him videos of both events. He'd explained, very politely but clearly, that being arrested twice, on trumped up charges, and tasered twice, by the same officer, was going to result in both a hefty lawsuit and a lot of unwanted publicity. The CC had spoken to his lawyers, then returned with an offer of £50k and an NDA.

'What is it with NDAs?' I asked.

'They help the world go round,' he told me. 'They smooth the way for law and order.' I snorted at this and he said, 'Don't knock it, little brother, if every lawsuit went to court, if every dirty sheet was washed in public, society would fall apart.'

'That twat has tasered me twice,' I said.

'He does appear... enthusiastic.'

'The word is not enthusiastic,' I said. 'The word is twat.'

He nodded. Then he said, 'Take the money. You aren't going to win against the Met. And the *twat* in question is not allowed to go near you. Ever again. I inserted that into the NDA. If he does, the agreement is voided and we sue them again.'

'Thankyou,' I said.

He pushed his plate to one side. 'Also, I've discovered why you keep getting arrested.'

'Have you? How?'

'I went to school with the Chief Constable. So did you, until you chose to leave the Oratory and attend Peckham High.'

'And.'

'He's a friend, distant, but we swap Christmas cards and the like: I've consulted for him in the past. He told me you've been consorting with a known terrorist.'

This was news to me.

'Of course, you may not have known that. In fact, I'm pretty sure you didn't.'

'I'm pretty sure I didn't either. Would you like to tell me who it is?'

'The man in the pub.'

I thought of my client from the airport, the one who wanted me to deliver a letter to someone whose whereabouts he didn't know. 'Him?' I said. He seemed too mild, too hesitant, too *quiet* to be a terrorist. A geography teacher, maybe. 'Doesn't seem the type. I don't know much about him,' I said. 'He wanted to hire me.'

'Don't tell me,' James warned. 'If you tell me I'll have to spill to the cops. But if it involves delivering heavy packages that tick, then I would suggest you turn him down.'

'Noted,' I said. 'But I really know nothing about him. I've only spoken to him twice.'

'He emailed you. Called you. Met up with you.'

'Yes,' I said. 'And some fucker bugged my house, then some Special Branch twat tasered me, twice. They could have just asked, I'd have told them.'

'So will you tell them?'

'Fuck no,' I said. 'Not now. I've run out of red carpet when it comes to the cops.'

'Keep your hair on,' he chided. 'I've found out a little bit about your mysterious friend. The reasons the authorities are so keen on getting in touch with him.'

'Do tell,' I said, sitting back.

'Your client. The one who managed to get you arrested and tasered twice.' He reached down to his briefcase and took out a file, set it out on the table top and opened it. On the inside was a 10x8 print. CCTV quality. Pixelated to the point where it was barely recognisable as a photograph of a human being. I took the picture, turned it round and studied it.

'Recognise him?'

'No.'

'It's the only picture the authorities have of the man you met in the pub.'

'It could be anyone,' I said, realizing he was wearing headgear both times I'd met him, and understanding now that that was probably not an accident. The figure in the photograph was walking through a city street that could have been New York, I could just about make out a Walk sign behind him: he was nondescript, dark pants, shirt, shoes, long dark hair and a straggly beard. The streets were shiny with rain and the person in the picture seemed to be alone. He was carrying a shoulder bag.

'Shortly after this picture was taken, a man called Moise Cassevetes was shot in the head with a .338

Lapua Magnum. The rifle, which we think was in that bag, was a...'

'Cassavetes collapsible.'

'Yes.'

'Aka the Murder Gun,' I said.

'The Assassin's Friend. The Night Caller. The Golf Bag Gun.'

'The nine iron,' I added. It had lots of names. The Cassavetes .338 was one of the few collapsible guns that could truly stake a claim to be being perfectly accurate. Mostly, the nature of a collapsible or folding gun meant that it wasn't as accurate as a static piece. Every part that slotted together or came apart, every screw that could be turned to lock something into place had a tiny but significant built-in margin for error, a tolerance that might be measured in mere thousands of an inch, but multiplied by a shot of say, four hundred yards, and you're talking three or four minutes of angle, which equates to missing the target. The Cassevetes, by virtue of a few interrupter-threads and a lot of precision-moulded polymer, was notorious for being one of the few guns that somehow managed to overcome the inherent inaccuracy of take-down guns, and give the user a flawless shot. One or two handmade guns maybe got better groupings, but they cost tens of thousands and the results were often patchy. The C338 was mass-produced and sold for less than fifteen hundred US dollars, and an averagely good marksman could hit a two-inch bullseye at six hundred yards over open sights. On top of that it was very light, being mostly polymer, with a built-in recoil system that discounted the heavy kick that you'd normally feel from a light, powerful weapon. Moise Cassavetes had designed the gun, he was an engineering genius, but he was also as business-minded as the most ruthless Wall Street trader too. His rifle was heavily promoted, easily available, and modular, so it encouraged customization and tinkering. It had earned him a fortune. He did for rifles what Gaston Glock had done for pistols, but he did it even better. Toward the end of my final tour of Afghanistan it had become the rifle of choice for the better class of talib sniper. Cassavetes had been killed about a year ago. Some said it was by the CIA, who were getting tired of the body count the rifle had quickly acquired, and wanted payback.

'You think this guy shot him.'

'It's not what I think, it's what the authorities think. There's more, here...' He took out another sheet and handed it to me. A list of names on a spreadsheet. Name. Nationality. Weapons designed. Weapons sold. Weapon that killed them. A lot of them seemed to be Germans, I noticed. Some American. A Dutchman. A Chinese. An Indian. But whatever nationality, they'd been killed by the weapons that they'd designed, or that had been marketed or sold by their companies. There was a company that ran an annual weapons festival in Hamburg, specialising in explosive devices. The owner and MD of this company was blown up while mowing his lawn by a landmine designed and built by his own company, and promoted at his own Expo. Or Explo, he'd called it, humorously. Posthumourously, I thought. I imagined him sitting on his mower, and for some reason he was wearing a Tyrolean hat and lederhosen, and then he was blown all to hell to the soundtrack of an oompah band. I smiled to myself for a moment as I visualised his Tyrolean floating back to earth, the jaunty feather smoking, as it settled on the cropped grass while oompah music played in the background. I wondered who had finished mowing the lawn. I read on. Others were not so whimsical. The designer of a polymer and porcelain combat knife that didn't show up on X-Ray was gutted by one of his own weapons. I read more, but I was getting the picture. Someone was killing arms industry moguls with their own gear.

'Why?' I said, putting down the sheet.

'I think the reasons are fairly obvious.'

'He's killing weapons designers with their own kit. I get that. But why?'

'Trying to make some sort of political statement?' James suggested.

'It's a very specific statement,' I said. 'Has he been in touch to say why he's doing it? Has he made demands?'

James shook his head. 'Not that I can find out.'

'None of this is in the UK,' I said. 'So why're Special Branch so keen?'

'I don't think they're keen on terrorists.'

'If all they want to do is lock up terrorists, they only need to round up the congregation of Finsbury Park Mosque.' I reached over for the file, slotted the sheet back inside, closed it. 'But this isn't about some brown kid from Bradford shooting some white kid from Cardiff in a side street in Kabul, is it?' I said. 'This guy is picking off members of the establishment. Someone is shooting the money.'

James nodded. 'The big international money-spinners are oil, drugs, human trafficking, and weapons,' he said as he closed the file, slotted it back into his briefcase. 'They think, previously, he was the man behind about twenty-five drug-cartel assassinations. In eighteen months, just about the entire south American drugs trade was decapitated.'

'Never heard anything on the news.'

'Cartels don't tweet.'

'I doubt the authorities were too upset.'

'They were ecstatic. Everywhere from Medellin to Ankara, major drug dealers were dropping like flies.' James paused as he slotted the file inside his briefcase. 'Then it went quiet. It seems, he moved onto slavers, both sellers and buyers, then arms manufacturers. And having done drugs, slaves and arms, they're worried at some point he'll move onto oil.'

'I bet they are.'

'Meanwhile, we have the coming visit of the Chairman of the CCP. You can imagine, the security boys are shitting bricks, and why they keep arresting you, they're desperate to find this guy but they don't know anything about him. And they think you do.'

'There could be repercussions,' I thought, saying it out loud. 'When everyone is ignorant, the slightest knowledge can be extremely valuable.'

'And dangerous.' James said. 'Special Branch might be the least of your worries,' his voice was calm and flat. 'Do you know anything about him, Mark?'

'Very little. I know what he looks like, that's all.'

'So you could ID him. Did you tell the police?'

'No.'

'Well as your legal advisor, I am instructing you to say nothing unless I am with you. Got that?'

I nodded. 'Thanks...'

'Don't call me bro.'

'...brother.'

He said, 'Seriously Mark, for the time being, I think you should get out of town. Think about the kind of people involved with the arms trade, human trafficking, drugs, the oil trade. Add in the Chinese, for whom a million deaths is a mere statistic. If any of them even suspect you know about this guy, if they suspect you know anything at all, they'll disappear you to some derelict, where they will find out what you know, and no one will discover your body. I'm very concerned.'

'I know. Thanks. But I have a contract that keeps me in town.'

'Fuck the contract.'

'I like to keep my end of the bargain. It's good money.'

'You're not broke, brother. I just got you fifty-grand for falling over in front of a Swat team.'

'I'm not sure where I could go.'

'What about that Latvian girl?'

'If I run abroad, they'll think I know something, and they *will* come after me. I'm not dumping my troubles in someone else's lap.'

'Her brother will protect you.'

Maybe. But no. I'm in their debt already, I can't bring them trouble again.'

'The New England girl?'

I thought of Beth Riley and her daughter, safe and happy and living in Ames, New Hampshire, and I thought of me dragging my troubles to their back yard. I shook my head. Not a chance.

'Have you got an ex on each continent?' he asked, mildly.

In reply, I looked him in the eye and just smiled, wanly.

'Maybe, if you hide, if you disappear, they'll think our mutual friend took you out.'

'And how long do I hide?' I asked.

'You hide until things go quiet, or they catch him. Or,' he added, knowing me well, 'Until you get bored.'

'It could be a long time before they catch him,' I said, ignoring his jibe, 'They don't know what he looks like; they don't even know his name.'

'Gun Jesus.'

'What?'

'It's what the Cartels called him. Gun Jesus. They said it's a story the cartel leaders would tell their acolytes, tell their kids, if you wronged someone, if you went back on your word, if you snitched, ratted someone out, did something against the code, Gun Jesus would get you.'

'They have a code?'

James shrugged.

'Gun Jesus?'

He nodded. 'No one knows who he is or where he's from. He's white, probably. European or American. Or Canadian. Or Australian. Or maybe middle-eastern, maybe Jewish. Ex-special forces, probably. Some say rogue CIA. Some say he *is* CIA.'

'But no-one really knows,' I said.

'No-one really knows,' he repeated. 'Except you. You sat with him, face to face.'

'I bought him a pint.'

'Don't. Even. Tell. Me.' He paused, 'You spoke with him. You can give a detailed description.'

'He didn't look like Jesus…'

'Don't tell me anything,' he repeated quickly, 'I'm your lawyer. If I know, and I don't tell, they can disbar me. Or kidnap me and torture me in your place.'

'Fair point.'

'You agreed to deliver something for him.'

'It wasn't a porcelain knife, or a .338 Cassavetes…'
I stopped.

I wasn't going to tell James anything. It wouldn't do any good to share, and he didn't want to know. I went back to the moment we met, the coffee we shared at the airport. *'You're a good man, Mark*

Barrett,' he'd said. He'd a friendly, open face; guileless, I'd have said. An honest face. Had he been playing me? Bringing me on board, forming a bond he could use to ensnare me, to keep me onside, to keep me from talking? To be fair, if some nefarious types tied me to a chair and began heating up a soldering iron, I wouldn't wait, I wouldn't hold out, I'd talk straight away. Tell them everything. I'd be telling enough for four volumes of an autobiography, five, if they got out the wire cutters. Maybe the guy from Heathrow, as I thought of him, was just chatting. Maybe there was no agenda on his part, beyond asking me to deliver a package, and chatting to me, the courier, like I'd say the occasional hello to the postman. But he had to know that, if coerced, I'd talk. I'd be like that truffle-shuffle kid on the Goonies, I'd bore them with the minute details of *every* little thing locked in my brain. There wasn't much to say, but I knew what little information I had could be very useful. I didn't know very much, but what I knew could help nail him. So why hadn't he killed me? If *I* was an international assassin, I'd kill all the witnesses, for sure. I looked up at James. 'Maybe I should get out of Dodge,' I said.

'I always envied you, you know.' James said as he stirred his coffee, 'Luke has his vocation, and I have my career, but we're both basically tied into a particular lifestyle and behaviour-set, whether we like it or not, no matter how much it chafes at times, whereas you, well you always did whatever you wanted to do…'

'The black sheep.'

'…I was going to say pirate.'

'Pirate?'

James nodded, 'The risk-taker, the headstrong one. When you left the Oratory and went across the river to Southwark, everyone thought you were mad, thought you might get killed.'

'I nearly did, once or twice.'

James smiled to himself, 'I was just envious of your ability to make a break. I thought, I know Mark's a fighter, but really? A posh boy from the Oratory going to a state school and mixing with all those,' he paused, thinking of a suitably PC word, '*gangsters*? But I was envious too. And I knew you'd be ok.'

It was my turn to smile. 'You meet more gangsters than me now.'

'I do, and a charming bunch of miscreants they are.'

'It gave me some callouses,' I said, 'Switching schools, leaving the Oratory and going to a state school. I needed them.'

'The man with the plan…'

'I never had a plan,' I admitted, quietly, like I hadn't really understood that 'til now.

'You always seemed like you knew where you were going,' he said.

'Really? I never knew where I was going,' I said.

'But you knew where you weren't going.'

This I had to concede. 'I couldn't be you, that's all. Or Luke. That's the only place I wasn't going. You. Or Luke.'

'No one can be like Luke.'

'I couldn't be like you either. My brother, the brilliant scholar. The intellect. The lawyer.'

'Sometimes I'd settle for less,' he said.

'Are we having a moment bro?' I said, a hint of tease in my voice.

'Oh, do fuck off,' he said, which made me smile. 'And don't call me bro. Or bruv. Or blad, or whatever they're saying in South Peckham these days.'

'Battersea,' I corrected. 'I live in Battersea.'

I studied James as he went back to stirring his coffee. He was dressed in a bespoke pin-stripe three-piece, his fitted shirt perfectly, his neat but understated tie, black with the thin red and white stripes. His shoes hand-made on Jermyn Street.

'You've done ok,' I said.

'I've done well,' he countered. 'Chambers at Temple...'

'A gorgeous wife,' I said.

'She is. Gorgeous.' He paused, and was about to say something, then he seemed to shift gear, 'She doesn't like you.'

'I know.'

'You're a threat,' he said. 'You're everything that's wild and disreputable and out of control.'

'She likes control, your bride.'

'She likes everything neat and tidy.'

'And I'm messy and unpredictable. Unlike you.'

'So, she thinks.'

'But we know better.'

A small grin. 'I'm happy with my life, Mark,' he said. 'I've always envied you your freedom. I don't *want* your freedom, he added, 'But sometimes, when I'm reading the eleventh book of the day searching for some wafer thin get-out-of-jail-free precedent that will aid a career-thug in his bid to escape the consequences of whatever violence he has inflicted on some unfortunate bystander, your lifestyle begins to seem carefree.'

The sandwiches arrived, hot and juicy, and we tucked in without another word. I ate military style, which was to say I stuffed it down as quick as I could manage without actually spilling any on my shirt. James ate his food slowly, savouring it. He'd never be allowed to eat a saveloy dip with all the extras in a greasy all-nighter if he was with his good lady wife. I reached over and picked up his napkin, 'Missed a bit,' I said, and he wiped his chin, a twinkle in his eye. While he finished off his food, I went back to the counter and ordered more coffee. I returned and set them down. 'So what's on your mind?' I asked.

'I've got a small job for you, if you want it.'

'You're brokering for me now?'

'No. The job is for me.'

'Go on then,' I said.

'How'd you fancy a trip to Canterbury?' James said. 'I may have a little job for you there, and it should be safer than London for a week or two. Maybe you could stay there afterwards, 'til things die down. And if your London contract crops up, you can get up here quick, do the job and disappear again.'

'Canterbury?' I said, 'That's where they murdered Thomas Beckett.'

'Unlike Beckett, you're no saint.'

'Beckett was a friend of Jesus,' I said. 'And so am I, apparently.' James said nothing, he was used to my failed attempts at wit and shrugged them off expertly. I leaned forward, 'So tell me about this job.'

Part 2

A Canterbury Tale

I removed the cartel bosses.

Their deaths were seen, in-house, as the cost of doing business. I concurred. If anything, the killing sprees that followed the power vacuum caused by my work did more damage than I ever could. No one on the outside took heed.
I moved on.

All I had was my mission, a growing ability to focus, and an uncanny knack of not being noticed. I put these to good use, and the body-count grew while I settled the karmic invoice.

Apart from a state-sponsored assassination of some political agitator eight hundred years ago, there wasn't a lot happening in Canterbury. And Thomas Beckett wasn't the first or the last cleric murdered by locals with a grudge, the place had been fairly mired in priests pursued by knife-wielding killers at one time or another. But now, apart from being home to the Primate of the Church of England, the place was sleepy and quiet. I stepped off the train and walked across the footbridge that took me from the platform and out to a half-filled carpark. I checked my mental map and turned right into town. What passed for 'town' was actually a few streets of pleasantly mismatched buildings, houses, the odd shop, and an occasional refurbished warehouse. There was a takeaway called Chop Chop, a half-timbered pub called the Unicorn and then another pub whose name I missed. I passed a church and took a left along London Road then another left until I was walking parallel to the direction I'd just travelled, but going the opposite way. No rush.

Eventually I came to the castle and walked up and along the soft turf moat that circled the wall, stared up at the grassy bailey, on top of which sat some greying stone monument. Intrigued, I walked until I found the entrance, went in and followed the path that led up the bailey until I stood at the very top, with the monument to my back, looking over the entire original town, just like the Norman baron who'd built the place might have done, nine hundred and fifty years ago. They had welcomed the Normans into Canterbury, back in 1066. They had close ties to the Church of Rome here, the Cathedral was within the castle walls, and they were more sympathetic to William's murdering psychopaths than they were to the murdering psychopaths of Harold Hardrada or Earl Godwin of Wessex. Canterbury was establishment, I thought, as I stared out from the hill where the castle had once stood, it was old establishment, and it had survived waves of invaders for thousands of years, from the Romans to the Romanians, with Viking hordes, the Spanish Armada, and the Luftwaffe in between. It had endured. This is England, I realised. It reminded me of Tolkien's' Shire. Sleepy. Comfortable. Secure. All I needed to see was some sturdy rotund guys in green and yellow clothes, with rosy cheeks and hairy feet. Maybe a wizard or two. I wondered if King Arthur was sleeping beneath this very hill, just waiting for the call. He'd be close by, I was sure.

An hour later I was sitting in a café opposite the Hilton Hotel. Watching for my target, a businessman name Davey Robson, a smooth-talking professional cockerney with a chain of car dealerships, selling everything from cheap Fords to new Aston Martins, with the odd Lambo chucked in for good measure. Davey.

I imagined some geezer in a wide-lapelled, doubled-breasted suit, slicked back hair, a car with a private number plate, wearing an expensive Rolex and cheap shoes. All I had for ID was a security badge head-shot taken for some trade junket that could have been a week old, or fifteen years. All James could tell me was that he was having an affair and he wanted some photographic evidence of that fact.

'Why not hire a private detective?' I asked.

'You're cheaper,' he said.

I hadn't asked why cost was an issue for a client who could afford James, a lawyer whose hourly rate was calculated in four figures. I should have, but I was glad of an excuse to get out of London. And maybe James was glad of an excuse to get me out of London too.

I texted James. *Mind if I book in the same place?*
He got back within seconds. *Receipt.*

I finished my coffee and sauntered across the road, booked in using the name on a fake passport, paid cash. The receptionist, a polish girl called Katerina eyed my luggage, which was a 20litre rucksack, and my clothes, which were hard-wearing but definitely not new. I thought of Davey and his shiny suit, and of other like-minded suit-wearing types who'd use this sort of place for business and illicit affairs, and I wondered if she had me down as aa typical euro-transient, which I guess I was, but she said nothing, just gave me the passkey and told me how to get to my room.

In my room I emptied my rucksack, showered and pulled on my training kit, went back downstairs and found the small gym advertised in the brochure I'd found on the bedside table – it consisted of a running machine, two kettle bells, an unloved punchbag that hung in one corner and lots of mirrors.
I got to work.
After thirty-minutes on the runner, I got off and did a session with the kettlebells. A slim woman wearing a fitbit, with a phone attached to her waistband and Bluetooth earbuds arrived and, after a brief warm-up, began using the running machine. Gym etiquette tells men not to stare at or bother women while they're training, it's like interrupting a priest during mass, a very attractive priest in this case, but I managed to ignore her and finished my kettlebells.
Then I stretched, properly, a fifteen-minute round of hamstrings, back, calves and every other part of me, and then I took my wraps and gloves from my gym bag, wrapped my hands and pulled on my mitts and attempted to hurt the punchbag that hung in the corner.
We all boxed as kids.
My eldest brother Luke is an ordained bishop of the Church of England, and he can punch the bag in a manner I can only describe as Foreman-esque: huge, stately punches that, if they connect, lead inexorably

to the opponent falling down. James, the next oldest, despite being quite skinny, has the hardest punch of the three of us. His hands are smart and he punches naturally, employing some sort of unearthly kinetic chain that builds naturally from the hips and results in tremendous and seemingly impossible power; the odd time I've seen him training, he hits so hard that others stop to watch. Me, I don't have Luke's destructive power or James' natural ability, which is why in a real fight I prefer to repeatedly smash my forehead into the bridge of someone's nose, something Greener once described, the first time he saw me do it, as a cross between a chainsaw and a woodpecker, but that was back in school, when I was learning to survive, and the furnace into which I'd leapt was turning my raw iron into spring-steel. To attempt that on a heavy bag would only lead to concussion, CTE or, at the very least, damage to my cervical discs, so I focused on my form and began punching, relaxed, and threw different combinations, remembering to move before, during and after each combo. I used different combinations, repeating them a hundred times each, jab/cross, jab/hook, low/high with the left, liver then jaw, then low/high with the right, spleen then jaw, going through as many combinations as I could. After a while I lost myself in the routine, the rhythm, the smack of gloved fist on bag, the shuffle of my footwork, the roll of my shoulders, thinking of the coach, Neil, at the gym we used to go to back when I was still at the Oratory, him shouting, 'don't just fukin stan' there, roll away! Hit and move! Move and hit! Footwork, Barrett. Foot. Work. Don't fukin embarrass me, get your fukin feet movin posh boy!'

When at last I was finished, looked round, the slim woman was gone. I'd been on the bag twenty hard, intense minutes and I felt it, especially round my back and shoulders, so I warmed down with ten minutes shadow boxing, worked on my form, practiced hitting from a no-guard: relaxed fence, standing oblique, hands out and slightly forward, palms up, hands wide, palms up, placatory, as though to say 'Wha?' then swinging my hands like I'd swing a baseball bat, torqueing my hips, relaxing my shoulder and letting it all go. It wasn't quite as perfect as James, or as powerful as Luke, but my intention was bad, and I knew it'd work. I'd known it to work. Finished, I went back to my room, took a shower and dressed for dinner.

Dressed for dinner is a stretch: I was kitted out like a wannabe Steve McQueen in chinos, sweatshirt and desert boots, eating reheated food in the restaurant of a chain hotel. The meal arrived, and it was cooked. I've had worse, but I've had a lot better too, and on many occasions. Most occasions. I chased the cooked chicken round the plate and finally gave up, deciding I'd find a takeaway and eat in my room. But just then Davey Robinson himself arrived in the hotel restaurant, and again, restaurant is a bit of a stretch, but it had tables and food, and now it had Davey Boy making himself comfortable at a corner table, so I stayed where I was, checked my phone, as everyone does, and ordered a coffee with cream, poured in heaps of soft brown sugar and waited.

I studied him. He wasn't what I expected, which was a cockney gobshite in a shiny suit. He was in his mid-thirties, tall and wide, but rangy in build, with a thatch of thick blonde hair. He was handsome too. I couldn't make out his words but I could hear his voice, which had the sort of shaved glass tones you only get from attending the best public schools. I had no doubt he had an apartment somewhere in the middle of West Kensington. I went back to my phone and wiki'd the company he worked for, discovered it was granddaddy's company, the old man had built the dealership from a post-war second-hand bike repair shop of dubious renown into a car dealership that spread across London and the Home Counties like Japanese knotweed. Father had dutifully taken over the business, and Davey and his siblings had been sent to St. Paul's and then straight into the family business. Sister Amelia was on the board, along with daddy, but Davey was not mentioned as being part of the management of the company. I glanced back at him, tall and wide and slim and relaxed and handsome. Too handsome to work as hard as you'd need to work to run a successful company. I guessed Davey wasn't much of a worker bee, he was the guy feasting on the manuka.

'So what do I do when I find this guy?' I'd asked James.

'Get evidence of him having an affair.'

'What, do I burst into his room to find him with a floosie, while wearing a trilby with a press badge slotted in the side and a guy with a woosh camera?'

'A what camera?' James almost laughed.

'You know, those old-fashioned cameras with the flash that goes "wooosh"'

'They used magnesium powder,' he said, 'But an iPhone will do.'

'And I get into his room how, exactly?'

'Doesn't have to be in bed. Just catch him with the woman in the hotel. Or somewhere else. They can be holding hands, kissing, whatever.'

'I'm a courier James. I'm not a detective.'

'You can be sneaky when you want to be.'

'I wouldn't call it one of my essential skills.'

'Do this job and I'll fund your trip to Canterbury.'

I sat back.

'For a month,' he added.

Christ, I thought. Canterbury for a month. That's not hiding out, it's a fucking pilgrimage. So I sat in the hotel restaurant and chewed on my meal, wondering if it would be wise to have my phone on the ready, just in case Ms. Floosie appeared and I could pretend to text while using my secret sideways camera to take pictures, though the way he was munching on his food suggested he wasn't expecting company, and after a while I went to the bar, leaving Davey boy to finish off his sausage and mash.

'How long's he down here for?' I'd asked.

'Two days, two nights,' James said.

'That's pretty specific.'

James nodded.

I didn't even know what room he was in.

In the Mission Impossible movies, Tom Cruise distracts the counter clerk while he spins the guest register and searches the list for the target. I didn't know how to do that. Sure, I could chat, I could flirt even, especially if it was the warm and friendly Katerina I'd met when I checked in, but how would I get her to leave her desk? Offer her money? Throw a rat onto the counter top? Where would I find a rat? What if she liked rats?

In the end I simply went and asked.

Katerina was still at the desk and I said, 'Can you tell me what room Davey Robinson is in?'

'Are you a colleague?' she asked.

'We're doing some business together,' I said, which was kind of true.

'228b,' she said.

'Don't tell him. I want to surprise him.'

'He's in the dining room,' she said.

'I know. I want to surprise him.'

She held my gaze for a moment longer than necessary. 'I finish at ten,' she said.

'I'll be finished with Davey by half nine,' I said.

'Take a shower,' she said. I realised that though I'd already showered after the gym, I was still glowing and perspiring. 'I'll come and see you,' she said.

It's funny how a little thing like that can lift your mood. I knew when to make my exit, so as not to spoil the moment, so I said, 'I'll order a bottle of wine.'

'I'll get the wine,' she said. 'I'll get the *good* wine.'

I thought to myself, you're coming to my room at ten, so any wine is good wine, but I composed myself and said, 'Right.' That left me a good three hours to do some detecting, or whatever they call it. 'Right,' I repeated.

Exit stage left.

On my way to my room I found a cleaner and asked if she could get me a folding chair. She raised an eyebrow at this but said nothing, got onto her walkie talkie and asked the porter to fetch one from the basement. When he delivered it to my room, I said thankyou, gave him a decent tip, and stacked it just inside the door. Then I showered again, cleaned my teeth, dressed, lay down on the bed and immediately fell asleep. I woke at quarter to ten and Katerina arrived, as promised, shortly after ten. Also as promised, she brought the good wine.

At four-thirty the next morning I unpeeled myself from Katerina's warm and enveloping form and dressed quietly in the dark. I picked up my phone from the dresser, and lifted the folding chair as I left the room. I walked along the carpeted corridor and then took the stairs until I arrived at the floor that Davey's room was on. I parked the chair at the end of a row of doors and sat down to wait. At six-thirty a porter appeared with newspapers and dropped them outside two of the doors. I asked him if he could get me a pot of coffee and some toast, told him my room number, and he nodded, and while he was gone I pinched one of the supplements to read. He didn't ask what I was doing. When he returned, I tipped him, as much for the coffee as for his silence. As I sat, drinking coffee, fending off sleep, reading the newspaper supplement, the world began to wake up. I could hear traffic outside, the faint whirr of a vacuum cleaner, noises of people moving about on the floor above. At seven-fifteen a guest left the room a couple of doors long from Davey's, and stared at me for a long moment at me. I looked up from the magazine, which really wasn't very good, and said a cheerful, 'Good morning.' He said the same back to me before getting into the lift, pulling his wheelie case behind him.

And then, at about seven twenty-five, the door to Davey's room opened and James' wife Clarissa stepped out. She stood there, fully clothed, but with her hair looking completely disheveled, like she'd been dragged through a bed backwards. I thought she wasn't going to see me but she turned, glanced along the corridor at me, and froze.

I looked at her and said, 'Morning, sis!'

Her expression turned to stone and then, almost like she had forced herself to *un*see me, she turned and went back into the room, shutting the door quietly. I was hoping she wouldn't come back out. I was hoping I could wait until Davey left, then go, and never have to speak to her. I realized why James had asked me rather than employ a detective: James was the client. I understood with awful clarity the trajectory of James and Clarissa's marriage and I just felt sad. Low. My brother, as big a pain as he could be, well he was my brother. The smart one. The intellect. Too sharp for me to ever feel comfortable around, and his wife was pretty much the same. I could have left.

I could have left and called James and said, 'It's exactly what you thought,' and left it at that. But I didn't. Because I thought, You can tell him, bitch. You can break the news of your infidelity to your husband, cos I'm not doing that to my brother. Of course, he knew already. He knew all along. He knew enough to name the actual time and place. He knew a lot more than me. Maybe he just wanted someone he could trust to confirm it. I wondered what she was telling Davey boy in there. I wondered if she'd fuck him one more time, just to make him malleable, to get him onside, wondered if that's what they were doing now. After another fifteen minutes, the door opened and Davey boy left the room, studiously not glancing in my direction.

So he knew too.

What now, I thought. Part of me was sitting watching this, enjoying the moment, curious as to what she would do, wondering if she'd plead, or threaten or, for one delicious moment, if she'd offer me herself as a bribe, as a way of keeping me quiet. Of course, I would magnanimously refuse, though I'd secretly savour the offer too. But instead, a few minutes after Davey left she left too, dragging a small case, not even looking in my direction. I watched her stop at the doors of the elevator and press the call button. After a minute or so the doors slid open and she went in, pressed a button, and as the door closed she turned and stared in my direction, as though she were staring at an empty corridor until the doors slid shut and she was gone. I sat there for a few minutes, staring at the closed doors. Then I stood, folded the chair and carried it back down to the dining hall, went to the counter and ordered breakfast. Because, in the absence of any other information, the army answer is to sleep, or eat. At this moment, sleep could wait. My stomach was calling.

Over scrambled eggs and mushrooms I went over my conversation with James and I quickly realized that he knew all along that his wife was having an affair. The question was, why send me? Why not just divorce her? It wasn't a money thing, she was as least as well off as he was, and they had no children so no one else's life was going to be screwed up. And if not divorce, why not at least confront her? And again, why me? She hated me? I was everything she despised, well, until it turned out she was doing that shit too. So maybe me sitting there, showed her to be a hypocrite, and she'd hate that, she'd be humiliated that I knew her dirty little secret – not the affair so much as the fact she was just like me – and every time we met up she'd know I knew, and she'd know that every air and grace she applied to herself was just so much face powder. It was concealer: I'd seen the ravages beneath. I realized then that James wasn't going to divorce her. He'd made his point. James might have had the hardest punch of anyone I knew, but he preferred strategy to flat out conflict. She'd return home, burning with shame, not at the affair, but at the fact that her despised brother-in-law knew her shit stank, just like everyone else's. And James would say precisely nothing. He'd maybe take her out for dinner tonight, parade her to his lawyer friends, encourage her to mingle and chat, and act as though nothing had happened. And he'd never mention it. Having me show myself to her as he must have known I'd do, that was enough. I took out my phone and texted him.

You twat.

I didn't expect a reply as I finished my eggs and had put my phone back in my pocket before I went for another coffee to wash down the eggs, but my phone buzzed as I made my way back to the table. It was Katerina, she was wondering where I'd gone and was offering herself in lieu of breakfast. As I'd already had the breakfast by this point, I felt having her too would be plain greedy. But I could be greedy.

'Ready?'

I looked up, Katerina was standing in front of me, dressed in civvies, looking healthy and flushed and happy, hoisting a duffel bag over a shoulder. I hadn't seen her in anything other than her hotel uniform or naked and now, in jeans and t-shirt and a wide smile she looked younger and more vulnerable, somehow.

A few minutes earlier I'd texted James: *leaving Canterbury, staying with a friend.*

And he texted back, *keep in touch.*

But he didn't ask where I'd gone.

I stood, pocketed my phone, and grabbed my rucksack. 'Let's go,' I said.

We left Canterbury and I felt I was one step ahead of Thomas Beckett; no one had treat my head like a hard-boiled egg and lopped off the top. Not yet, anyhow. An hour later we were parking her car on a sleepy side road in a tiny village called St. Michael's, which seemed to be a series of modern housing estates set scattered around a pre-war village, itself dotted with the evidence of a much older hamlet. The street signs told me it was part of the borough of Tenterden but it felt like the original village was probably older than the castle at Canterbury; it was like that in a lot of places round here - though many of the houses were quite new, the narrow lanes between were deep and shaded and indefinably ancient. Katerina cranked the handbrake on and turned off the engine. I looked up at the house she'd told me she shared with three friends. It was small and irregular, built with the sort of longer, flatter bricks that hadn't been popular since Dickens' time; they were darkened in a way that suggested it preceded Dickens by at least a century. She got out of the car and I followed, grabbing both our bags, studying the surroundings carefully without really thinking about it, just a long-formed habit I couldn't shake, then I walked up to the front door where she was bent over and raking beneath the doormat for the key. 'We only have one,' she told me, pushing her hair back from her face. She unlocked the door and we went inside. 'We share it,' she explained. Then she showed me round the house, which took about eleven seconds, then took me upstairs to her room, which was tiny, and her bed, which was even tinier. I could grow to like St. Michael's, I thought as she dragged me down onto the firm mattress.

I'd been awake since four, and hadn't had much sleep before that, so that when she was finished with me, I slept a deep, dreamless sleep. It's rude, I know, to sleep soundly in a woman's bed, when she's awake and bustling, but I'd learned to take my rest where I could. About four in the afternoon I woke feeling refreshed though slightly thick-headed, and Katerina must have heard me moving about upstairs, she came up and showed me where the bathroom was. When I'd showered, shaved and changed, I thoroughly cleaned away any mess I'd left in the tiny bathroom. I'm a bloke and sometimes it seems that blokes can get away with leaving a mess in a girl's bathroom, but I'm ex-Army too, and leaving a bathroom belonging to four women littered with shaving foam and dirty razors wasn't big and it wasn't clever. Then I went downstairs to find her facetiming; she glanced up and raised her brows quizzically in such a way that I immediately shut up and made myself invisible and she went back to her conversation and continued to speak rapidly in Polish to some bloke on the other side of the screen. For a moment I felt bad and reflexively I glanced at the third finger of her left hand to check there wasn't a ring, there wasn't, so I relaxed a little and thought to myself, all's fair, etc.

'We're going to the pub, coming?'

'Sure,' I said.

Katerina and her friend Evie had spent an hour or more getting ready, leaving me to sit alone in the living room, and now they were already at the door ready to go out. The subtle shift from Katerina and me to Katerina and Evie, and the fact she used 'we' told me that after about eight hours in this pleasant little house, my time was almost up. 'Can I catch you in about thirty minutes?' I said, 'got to phone a couple of people at work.' Evie looked dubious about the prospect of leaving this complete stranger in her home, but Katerina had seen my credit card when I registered at the hotel and I guess she thought me trustworthy, and she said 'That's fine,' we'll see you at The Crown.'

I had no intention of staying at Kat's that night. It's not that I wanted to run out on her after spending best part of a day being extremely intimate with her, but Evie wasn't keen, and this was their house. Kat and Evie would be friends long after I'd gone. I'd go to the Crown and have a drink, make my excuses and then my exit.

When they closed the door, I went upstairs and washed, changed into clean underwear, but kept the same t-shirt, jeans and Steve McQueen boots, stuffed my jacket into my rucksack and pulled on a hoody. I cleaned my teeth using my own brush and some toothpaste I found in the bathroom cabinet, had to lean a little to get under the eaves of the roof to see myself in the mirror and check I hadn't got toothpaste on my chin. I went into Kat's room, repacked my bag, hoisted it and went downstairs, switched off the lights and left, slamming the door behind me.

The Crown was about a half mile away, they'd drove together in Kat's mini, but I walked it in an easy ten minutes. I stopped outside and texted Greener, and then I ordered a taxi for nine. I went inside and bought myself a drink. The pub was empty, apart from a couple of locals by the bar, and the two girls who were sitting in a booth. I glanced across at where they were sitting. Kat smiled nervously, Evie was frosty. It was a girl thing, I thought, territory, friendship, something like that; I'm a neat and respectful guest but some people just don't like strangers appearing in their home. That'd be me too, I thought, if someone brought a stranger back to my place. I took my drink over and sat down.

'Hey,' Kat said.

'Hey.'

Evie stood and went to the bar.

'We need to talk,' Kat said quietly.

'Ok.'

'Evie isn't happy with you staying over. Says she doesn't know you.'

'She doesn't,' I said. 'I could be anybody.'

Kat said nothing.

My phone buzzed in my pocket, so I took it out and answered. Greener spoke, 'This is your Personal Escape Plan Service,' he intoned, like a bad impression of Arnold Schwarzenegger, 'Jacob Greener at your disposal.'

'Greener,' I said, pleased to hear his voice.

'Where are you, man?'

'St. Michael's.'

'Where?'

'Tenterden.'

'Where?'

'Kent.'

'Ok. Need picking up?'

'Like you're going to drive to Kent to pick me up,' I replied, a smile on my face.

'Mate, I wouldn't drive across Peckham High Street to pick you up,' he said, a broad grin in his voice. I looked at Kat, studied her thick chestnut hair, almond eyes and high cheekbones that were a genetic echo of some Hun ancestor, and the soft, full mouth that was all her own. 'I have to go man, call you back in a bit.'

He hung up and I put away my phone.

'Work?' she asked.

'Yes. Got to go back to London.'

'Tonight?'

'I'm a courier. They got a job for me.'

I lie, smoothly.

She nodded, slowly, guessing the lie, despite the smoothness. 'It's been lovely,' she said.

'You've been lovely,' I told her. I turned to look as a few more people arrived noisily in the pub, and then I stood and went to the gents, figuring that'd allow Kat to fill Evie in on the good news. The corridor was narrow and dark, the toilet tiny, and on my way back to say goodbye to Katerina and her pal, I had to pause to let the two guys who'd been sitting at the bar squeeze past me.

Violence is a strange thing.

Sometimes you know stuff, even when you don't, cos I knew things had just gone bad a millisecond before one of the two guys tried to swipe me with a lead-filled cosh, and I was already flinching to my right so that the cosh swung through empty air and he fell forward slightly with the follow-through, and I twisted round and punched him in the neck so that he crunched forward with a cough, then I kicked him in the chest, aiming for his solar plexus and missing but feeling the crack of a rib. Then I stepped back, deciding what damage to do him next, which gave his friend a spare moment to hit me with his own cosh. Not good, I thought, as my conscious mind parted company with my body, and I dropped like a plank, noticing, as if from some weird distance, that I vibrated for a second or two as I lay on the floor. And as I lay there one of them kicked me in the head, and things went even more fuzzy, something shifted in my head – maybe time, maybe a blood clot, I couldn't be quite sure - but the next thing I knew, I was sitting against the wall in the same narrow corridor, my vision still blurred, and a stranger was checking to see if my bones were in the correct places. The two assailants were gone, but I saw what I thought were blood smears on the wall, and a spatter pattern running across the door, glistening maroon in the weak light. This new guy, whoever he was, pulled me into a siting position, slapped my face a bit and told me, 'You're alright.'

'I'm alright,' I said, noting my voice slurring, getting to my feet feeling like someone who had been coshed and then kicked in the head. I lurched back along the corridor, my feet unsteady, opened the door and headed back into the bar while the room swayed on either side of me. No one had noticed a thing. The pub was filling up now, music was playing, Kat and Evie were chatting happily, as I made it back to the booth. I picked up my rucksack, 'Got to go,' I said, and without waiting for a reply I wobbled my way to the exit and went outside into the street and the fresh night air and sat down heavily on a wall that separated the pub from a takeaway next door. I don't know how long I sat there but eventually I heard a voice. The voice spoke again. I could hear screams inside the pub now. Then the voice spoke a third time. 'Taxi for Barrett?'

I stood up.

'You Barrett? Tenterden Station?'

'Yes.'

'You drunk?' the taxi driver asked, dubiously.

'Concussed,' I managed to whisper, 'I think.'
'What's happening in there?' the taxi driver asked, the shouts and screams were audible. In reply, I opened the taxi door and sat on the back seat.
'Every fucking week,' he muttered, 'Fighting every week.'
'Seems like a nice place,' I murmured as he got in, started the engine and pulled away drove, and me looking at the houses, some neat Lego boxes, others old and higgledy. He glanced back at me. 'You ok mate?' but his voice seemed like it was coming from the other end of a long tunnel. Then the world went black.

I found out later that the taxi driver drove me to the hospital. Later, I called him to thank him and pay him too, and he said I didn't smell of alcohol and I was out of it, and at first, he drove toward the station thinking to just unload me there, but when I began choking on my own tongue he administered first aid and drove me direct to casualty. The kindness of strangers. I should make the effort to remember that cabby, and be kind in turn to people who need my help, but I don't know that I will. I'm not always kind. Either way, I ended up in a hospital bed with concussion that combined with the still-lingering after effects of being tasered twice to make me feel soft and woozy. I woke the next morning, and around eleven, a doctor checked me over, asked,

'What happened?'

'Think I got jumped.'

'I think you did. Any pain.'

'Headache,' I said.

He nodded, 'We think you were struck across the head...'

'Lead-filled blackjack.'

'You remember?'

'I remember the blackjack,' and I squinted as the memory brought on more pain.

'We should contact the police,' he said.'

'The taxi driver,' I said, 'Did I pay him?'

'I don't know.'

'I reached for my phone, checked the number I'd called for the taxi the night before, guessed there'd be no one around at ten in the morning and decided to call later, noticed there were five texts from Katerina, ranging from *What the fuck happened*? to the more charitable, *Are you all right*?'

'You have a mild concussion,' the doctor said. He smiled. 'But you seem to be doing fine. We'll run some tests in an hour or two.' He wrote some notes then left. A nurse arrived and sat me up. A while after the brief excitement of being manhandled by a portly female in uniform, the tea lady came around and I got a cuppa too. The wonders of the NHS. A while after that I felt a bit clearer, so I texted Katerina that I was all right, asked what happened after I left.

She texted back *You staggered out like you were stoned, then someone found two guys who had been battered unconscious, lying in the yard behind the toilets. Was that you?*

No I texted back. *I think they jumped me first. Someone else got involved. I was out for the count. Whoever it was that got involved, he left a bit of a mess.* Then she asked, *where are you?*

Hospital bed, I almost replied, but then deleted it before I sent it. *London*

She didn't reply.
I messaged Greener *I need a lift.*
He got back to me *Where are you?*
Not Peckham I replied.

Tenterden hospital is a bit pushed for beds and one fit-enough bloke with a headache does not equate to a bed for two nights running, so they didn't argue too much when I signed myself out.

I was sitting just inside the entrance when I saw a black Beemer roll up and flash its lights. I grabbed my rucksack and went out. A tinted window slid down and a stranger asked, 'Mark Barrett?'

'Yeah.'

'Greener sent me to pick you up.'

I must have looked a bit dubious. 'He told me to tell you he definitely lost that bet back in year nine.'

Only Greener would know that piece of our shared history. Though I'm still convinced I won the bet. I dumped my bag in the back and climbed in beside the driver. The car was a big old 5 auto, leather seats and an engine that would go round the clock three times if treated with anything less than sheer contempt. 'Belt up,' he said, so I did, and less than an hour later we were approaching the Congestion Zone.

He dropped me at my front door and I got out.

'Thanks pal,' I said, which were the only two words I'd said since I got in.

'No worries,' he said, winding down the window to watch me go.

I stopped, asked, 'You a relative of Greener?'

He nodded. 'Everyone's a relative of Greener.'

'Thanks again.'

He nodded and pulled away. I stood for a while thinking, 'What day is it?' and wondering where I'd left my door keys. In the end I walked along to Zed's cornershop and picked up my spare, reminding myself to get another set cut as soon as.

I resolved not to get beaten up ever again and slept most of the rest of the day. I woke the next morning around half-six, feeling fresh, with only a latent ache at the back of my head. I stretched and did a quick workout that consisted of stretching, crunches and kettlebells then I checked the fridge but what little was there was out of date so dressed quickly and went back to Zed's again to buy bread and milk and some pre-packed cheese, then went home and breakfasted while checking my mail and listening to the news while I ate. No messages from my brother the lawyer. I wondered what he was up to, if he was playing some chess-game with his spouse. He was, I knew. I was merely a gambit in his game. A sacrificed pawn. I finished my cheese on toast wondering why cheap cheese tasted better than the expensive stuff? A little voice answered that it was because of all the carcinogenic preservatives and flavourings, but I ignored that voice. There were three emails from customers, the first a thankyou and a possible recommendation, the second a complaint that the painting I'd delivered just wasn't very good. I couldn't make out whether this was dryly humorous or just plain weird. You don't complain to the postman because the sweater you bought on eBay doesn't fit. Or maybe you do. I deleted it. The third was from someone claiming to represent Tim Lord, eccentric billionaire, visionary and inventor, which I deleted. Then I sat back and closed my eyes. Canterbury had been... interesting. Not to be repeated, though there'd been some good moments. I was not cut out to be an exile from my beloved city: I might leave her for a day or two, but I'd always return.

Part 3
Gun Jesus

The slavers were the easiest to kill.

A man comfortable torturing women and children, comfortable selling human lives, is a man easy to kill. A man who should die, badly.

I was imaginative: piano wire, immolation, a stiletto through the perineum, interred in a container, or simply trussed and then handed over to their victims for reparation.

They recognised my handiwork, in which I acknowledged theirs.

'My shout,' Jarvis said.

We were back in the same pub, round about the same time. 'If you keep working this hard, you're going to get cirrhosis,' I told him when he returned with two foaming jugs of beer.

'It's a tough job,' he said, sitting down, 'But someone has to do it.'

'Cheers,' I said.

'Ditto,' he said, raising his glass and downing at least a third in one swallow.

'So,' I said, 'Business or pleasure?'

He put his glass down onto the table with a bang. 'Purely business.'

I took a slower drink from my glass, put it on the table opposite his and said, 'Fire away.'

He winced at my turn of phrase. 'This comes from way above me, I'm just the messenger.'

'And...?'

He wiped his mouth, 'That bloke you were working for.'

'Gun Jesus,' I said, and he winced again but nodded. 'We're after him, now, and in a *serious* fashion. We need him found and we need him in a cell, asap.'

'I'll do whatever I can,' I said.

'I know. We need all the information you have. Where and when he contacted you. All emails and other comms. Full description. Everything.'

'Ok,' I said. 'Now?'

'You'll spill?' He seemed surprised.

'You just had to ask nicely.'

He took out his phone, turned on the camera, placed it against an empty glass on the table and said, 'Now.'

I gave him the full description, all the information I had. It didn't take long. 'I'll forward you the emails and texts,' I said, and seeing his expression, added, 'I'll do it now.' I opened the mail box on my phone and quickly forwarded all the comms between me and Mr. Herr. Tom checked he'd got it and said, 'Anything else.'

'That's it, but if I do think of anything else, you'll get it straight away.'

'He wanted you to deliver a package?'

'Yes.'

'Did you get it?'

'I was in the middle of talking to him when your friends turned up at my flat. I left him without concluding our business.' This was all true, but it wasn't everything. I didn't mention the package my neighbour Millie had given to me. After a few days of it sitting on my shelf, I'd taking the precaution of giving it back to Millie and asking her to look after it for me, figuring that, otherwise, someone was bound to steal it long before I ever got it delivered. So, out of sight etc. Tom studied me for a moment. Then he switched off the phone camera and put it back in his pocket.

'Are you going to kill him?' I asked.

'We'd prefer to just stop him killing anyone on UK territory,' Tom said. 'He's a mission-orientated serial killer and, to be honest, if I had the choice, I'd like him to come work for us, but that's not going to happen, he only kills bad guys, and we spend a lot of time cosying up to bad guys, especially the ones with money.' He took a long drink from his glass.

'Bean counter politics,' I said.

'He's a moral murderer. We'd just like him to take his morality elsewhere.'

'He's still in the UK?'

'He was when you met him.'

'He might have gone.'

'He might be here for a reason,' Tom said.

I thought again of the package he'd sent me.

Tom said, 'Xao is due in a couple of weeks.'

'You think he's the target?'

'We have to assume he is, even if he's not.' Tom finished his pint. 'I fucking hate politics. I've spent the last week liaising with a Major from the Chinese close protection team.'

'I bet that's fun.'

'Working in tandem with humourless Chinese secret fucking police, protecting an absolute twat from the righteous repercussions of his own twattish actions, on behalf of the useless clowns who run this great and good nation. What's not to like?'

'It's a tough job,' I said again. He raised his empty glass. 'I'll get them in,' I said, rising to go to the bar. 'Get me a chaser too,' Tom said.

Fuck, I thought. It's barely lunchtime and he's on the whiskey. It must be serious.

With the money I'd gotten from the cops, I was in no serious hunt for work, but work arrived anyway. I got a call to pick up a small but valuable piece of art from an apartment on Kensington High Street late on Tuesday evening. I arrived, knocked on the door, and was met with blank looks by the person who answered. Nope. Not here, he said.

Some joker had sent me on a wild goose chase. I thought it might be the cops having a laugh, or the goons from Special Branch, with whom I'd formed a mutually antagonistic relationship over the last few weeks. I left the motorbike parked where it was and walked along the road to get myself a coffee. MaccyDs was busy but not packed, about half the customers were cycle delivery types, picking up orders for people too lazy to come and fetch it themselves. I ordered a large coffee and a chocolate brownie, took a window seat and watched the traffic. It was threatening rain and I thought I should get home in the next hour or so. I took out my phone and checked for emails. Nothing. Being a courier is like being a soldier. It involves lots of time sitting around, mixed with odd moments of highly-focused action. The difference is that couriers don't get killed. Usually. I read the news on my phone: lots about the forthcoming visit of Xao, some stuff about the failures of the current American President, and something about veterans of the War on Terror suing the American and British governments, a shootout in Chinatown, which made a change from the usual drive-by in Peckham. I put away my phone, took the lid off my coffee, and concentrated on the snack in front of me. The door opened and someone in cycling gear came in and went to the counter, chatted to the staff, then walked over and sat at the seat beside me. I glanced at him.

I glanced at him again.

Mr. Herr.

'I'm very sorry for the trouble I've caused you, Mr. Barrett,' he said.

I took a deep breath, shook my head at our strange, tangential relationship, and the trouble it was causing me. 'People are searching far and wide for you,' I said, 'Indicating his cycling outfit. Turns out, all they had to do was order a pizza and they'd get you arriving at their door.'

He smiled. 'What have you heard about me?'

I closed the lid on my coffee. 'That you're a man on a mission.'

He nodded slowly. 'I was.'

'Was?'

'I'm planning to retire,' he said.

'You should speak to my pal Tom Jarvis. He'll be very pleased to hear that.'

'Would he believe me?'

'No,' I said. 'But he'd settle for you leaving the country. Would you like a coffee?'

'I can't stay,' he said. 'I came here to apologise to you.'

'You paid me,' I said. 'No need to apologise, but, I accept it. Thanks.'

'I've arranged for an extra payment, for your troubles,' he said.

We both turned as a crowd of kids walked in, loud and lairy, and waited a few moments before continuing. I said, 'You're retiring?'

'I've done enough.'

I thought of the organiser of the Explo, killed by an exploding lawn mower, his Tyrolean hat drifting slowly onto the grass, feather smoking. The knife maker killed with his own blade. The riflemaker shot by his own gun. The cartels. The slavers. I nodded, 'You've probably done your share.'

'Thankyou again,' he said, and we chatted for a few minutes about his imminent retirement. Nothing specific, he just told me he'd done enough and wanted out. Then he said goodbye and stood, quietly, smoothly and without another word he left. I watched him go outside, mount a cycle and disappear into the darkness. Part of me, most of me, expected that at any moment the cops would arrive mob-handed, then taser me, and my heart began to race in anticipation, but they didn't, so after ten minutes, I finished my snack, threw the rubbish into the bin, went back out onto the High Street, walked back to my venerable 850T, dragged on my helmet and gloves, fired it up, and rode home. When I got back to Battersea, May was waiting outside. Despite being wrapped in a huge coat she was visibly shivering. 'Hey, come in out of the cold,' I said, after I turned off the engine and removed my helmet. 'Thankyou,' she said, smiling up at me, even her lips were shivering.

I pulled up the collar on her jacket, kissed her lightly on the nose and said, 'Come on in.'

The next day was blowy and chill, the first signs of the end of summer, and I spent a couple of hours with my accountant. Yes, I have an accountant who ensures that I keep my relationship with the Inland Revenue squared away, that I keep track of all my expenses, and don't get jailed for tax evasion. I have a difficult relationship with law enforcement so I ensure that whatever happens, they don't Capone me due to a lax approach to receipts. After his usual lecture about how I should run a company car and stuff like that, he gave me a clean bill of health, reminded me to keep a record of my expenses, and sent me bushy-tailed back into the world of commerce.

When I got home, May was gone, leaving me another of her business cards, this one featured a cartoon of a small pile of books and a sad face. I wondered where she got these cute cards. I might get some. My phone number, alongside a cartoon image of a broken-down motorbike might be good. Or one of those smileys with the XXs for eyes linked by a curly wire to a taser. I spent what was left of the morning doing personal admin, which is army code for tidying up, cleaning the house and bagging off my dirty washing.

I was at the launderette when Wookie found me, later in the day. He walked in like he owned the place, sat down beside me and said, 'Barrett.'
'Wookie.'
'That tech you gave me,' he said without preamble.
'Yeah?' I watched the washing machine as the clothes tumbled. It was calming.
'Most of it was standard British issue.'
'You said.'
'Two of them were not.'
The machine stopped its cycle and beeped three times. I stepped up and pressed the 'spin' button. After a moment's pause it began to whirr. I sat back down. 'And?'
'They're top grade. Tiny. Very high quality.'
I watched the machine spinning the water from my clothes.
'Chinese.'
'The bugs?'
He nodded. 'Everyone thinks Chinese stuff is shoddy, and the stuff they sell on the open market sometimes is, but the kit they produce for themselves is top notch. I've only heard of this gear, never seen it before. Had to send it to a pal to confirm the origin.' He waited, but when I said nothing he said, 'You checked that camera yet?'
I shook my head. 'Forgot all about it.'

'Man, you'll never make a spy. Here.' He handed me a USB.

'What's this?'

'I checked it for you?'

'You checked the camera in my living room?'

'Someone had to. I scrolled past the naughty stuff. You should see the rest of it.'

'I will.'

The spin cycle ended and I went to open the washer door. I turned to Wookie. 'Should I be grateful for you spying on my house?'

'No one likes a guard dog, Barrett. Until the bad guys arrive. Check the USB when you get home. When this is all done I'll remove the spy-cams.' He smiled, got up and left. I looked through the misted windows and saw that it was raining outside. I put my still-damp clothes into the dryer, pressed the buttons, and waited.

I got home, put my clothes on a rack to air out, went downstairs and worked on the bike for a couple of hours. The rain was drumming on the basement window as I worked on the ancient 844cc transverse V-twin engine. I hadn't quite sorted out exactly why it kept shutting out when I leaned into a right turn, but I figured I'd find out sooner or later, or die when the bike cut out mid-turn, with a Sainsbury's delivery truck on my tail. The music coming from the old speakers I'd wired from upstairs rigged kept me happy as I worked, and a couple of hours passed, until the heavy clouds and the drawing-in of the day made it a bit too gloomy to work on the fiddly bits. I put it back together, cleared every away, gave it a quick polish and set my tools back in the box, then switched off the light as I walked back up the stairs. As I washed the grime from my hands, I remembered the USB that Wookie had given me. I made a coffee and sat down at the kitchen table, plugged it into my laptop to see what was on it, hoping he hadn't downloaded the shenanigans that May and I had got up to in the living room. The USB opened to show a low-lit but clear image of my living room, and the time, which was 2.27am. Last night. My memory of that time was nil, as May had worn me out by a half past midnight, and I'd slept the rest of the night. At 2.29am the door opened and May stepped into the living room. She sat down at my computer, the one I was looking at now. The image shifted to the view from the laptop camera, of May's face, concentrating as she keyed in whatever, to whoever. It took a couple of minutes, but Wookie had helpfully enclosed a transcribed account at the foot of the screen of what she was doing. She'd searched all the files I'd opened in the previous month, then checked my email account, at which point I realised that she had my password for both. Then she'd used a USB to download a copy of everything on the computer, which took a couple of minutes. Wookie's narration explained that she'd also uploaded a trojan which would monitor my every activity, online or not. In brackets, Wookie told me that his USB was trojan-proof. I watched for a few more minutes. The view switched from the laptop camera to Wookie's wall camera, and I watched her close the lid, then leave the room, presumably returning to the warmth of my bed. The final part of Wookie's commentary told me not to use this laptop, or my phone any more. He'd be around at 8pm to swap them over for replacements that would look the same. I closed the lid, closed my eyes, and not for the first time I was grateful that I had Jacob Greener for a friend. He was always putting out for me, and the reason he did, he said, was that I was one of those low-chance, high-reward types. He'd probably help me out forever and get nothing in return, but there was a small chance that one day I might come through on something big. And on that day, he'd be ready to earn a proper commission. But that was just Greener avoiding the real reason he helped me so often.

He was my friend.

My beneath-the-streetlamp meetings with Wookie were becoming a thing, I thought, as he took my laptop and phone and handed over the replacement gear. 'I've never known anyone get bugged the way you have. You been upsetting people?'

'Someone I met,' I said.

'Best stay clear then. If they want you out of the way they can find a dozen ways to disappear you: jail, hospital, or just, well,' he paused and grinned, 'You know.'

I nodded.

'Thanks, Wookie. I owe you.'

'Just give me the kit when you're done. It's top of the range, I can make a decent return selling it.'

'Deal.'

He looked at me. 'Seriously Barrett, watch your back. You're entering a world where normal rules don't apply.'

'I'm not even sure how I got into it.'

Wookie slotted the gear into a rucksack as I spoke. He looked back at me, 'You ever been jumped?'

'More than once.'

'Did you waste time complaining, or did you fight back?'

It's in my nature to fight back. I smiled, slowly, realizing what he was suggesting. 'Right,' he said, turned to a car that sat idling nearby, and nodded. The lights turned on and it quietly rolled towards us. I went back inside, shut the door behind me, sat down on my comfy living room chair, leaned over and switch off the lamp. In the darkness I tried to work out how to fight back. Truth was, I didn't even know who I was fighting.

Weirdly, knowing that May was spying on me just made her seem hotter. It's a bloke thing, I guess, but knowing our 'relationship' was purely transactional, albeit for reasons unknown to me, made everything that much more intense. It was like that situation where an ex contacts you for a one-off booty call and because you know it's nothing long-term, because you know that the acts you share have no deeper meaning than the acts themselves, it can get extremely hot and dirty, extremely quickly. It was great, but we did some stuff that left me feeling grubby. It only took an hour for May to sussed it.

'You've changed,' she said, abruptly, as we lay together after a particularly intense bout of international relations. 'You're not *you*.'

'What am I then?' I asked.

'Someone *horrible*,' she said.

'You didn't seem to mind.'

Her expression went blank and she got out of bed, went into the bathroom. An hour later she was dressed and finishing off the last of the coffee-pot.

'How long have you known?' she asked, looking up when I entered the room.

'A couple of days.'

She pursed her lips.

'You work for the CCP,' I said.

'Every Chinese works for the CCP.'

'You're not a student?' I felt stupid asking this basic question.

'I *am* a student,' she told me, her voice short with emotion. 'But they ask,' and she paused, looked up at me, a sad smile, 'They ask,' she repeated. 'And we do.'

'Got to love those dictatorships,' I said. 'They get things done.'

She looked past me. Her expression opaque.

'I'm sorry,' I said.

'Me too,' she said, her eyes beginning to shine, but still not looking at me. She stood up, came to me and gave me a brief, intense hug. She had a tiny, frail body, and she quivered with emotion. Then she let go turned and walked out of the kitchen, out of the flat, and out of my life. So much for fighting back, I thought, staring at the kitchen door. I just took it out on a girl. I felt grim. I felt like a scrub. I picked up my phone and messaged Wookie: *I want a deep clean. I want this place sterile. I don't care if you tear the place apart, brick by brick. You can keep everything you find and I'll pay you on top of that.*

He arrived within an hour, with his team, and a van full of electronic gizmos. I left him a spare key and told him to call me when it was done. Standing below the lamppost, my new office it seemed, I went through my emails, found the message I was looking for, and sent a message in return, then I walked towards the Tube station.

The norns are fickle, the Valkyries ever vigilant. If caught, there would be no preamble, no trial, no lengthy sentence. I took pause. Where better to end this, I realised, finally, than in the company of the man who gave me this chance?

I didn't get a reply. I thought maybe he'd used the email address once and discarded it. In the meanwhile, Wookie pronounced my flat clean of bugs, and I went back in and cleaned up. The bed smelled faintly of May's scent, so I took off the sheets, balled them up and binned them. I opened the window to let the rain-swept London air clear away the residual scent. Then Ruby texted me to tell me that the scare was over. Their 'person of interest' had been spotted getting off a flight in Schipol. Gun Jesus had scarpered back to Europe.

It was over.

Mentally I reviewed the events of the previous few weeks. It had been an interesting time: I'd turned down the offer from the ministry, and the money they'd offered, which meant I couldn't get my flying licence back, but it was too late for a rapprochement between the army and me. Being tasered by the cops, twice, had made me fifty grand better off, and then some, which made me smile, though I wasn't sure the long-term effects on my grey matter would call that a win. Then a trip to Canterbury, I slid past the memory of being knocked senseless in a pub, and what I'd discovered in the hotel on behalf of my brother, focused on the good moments. I'd had a few good runs on my bike. Not a bad summer. But I needed to stop getting in trouble, I thought. No one can survive this level of physical trauma on a regular basis. I thought of May and felt sad. All Chinese work for the CCP, she'd said. They ask, we do. I wanted to believe she'd cared for me, even just a little bit; her reaction to our last lovemaking had shown she felt something, even if it was bad.

Still, there was no reply to my email.

I figured he'd dropped that particular mailbox as a communication method. The truth was, after all the excitement, I was suddenly at a loose end and was looking for something to keep my mind occupied, but my friendly international assassin had disappeared along with gainful employment. I didn't need the money, but I did need something to keep me busy. I thought of May again and felt low, again.

A week passed.
Then a month.
Then two months.
I'd begun to dislike my home and was spending a lot of evenings sitting in Costa or MaccyDs or Starbucks, reading endless newspaper articles and shit novels of derring-do, watching Fast & Furious movies and re-runs of the Wire and the Sopranos on my laptop. Autumn was in full flow, it rained a lot, and I was enjoying the darkness more than the light. And so it

was, not being home, I missed a couple of visitors, and only found out much later when Millie told me. Sitting at a Costa window seat one wet October evening, I read in a newspaper that the visit of Premier Xao, who's previous visit had been unaccountably postponed, was now due in about a week. I imagined various security services changing out of their pissed their pants, having recovered from over their inability to find a single person in the most CCTV'd city on earth: North Korea has nothing on London when it comes to spying on its citizens, but they hadn't managed to find him. Another evening, I went down a google rabbit-hole, reading a series of articles on our inelegant ejection from Afghanistan. As a soldier I knew that it was pointless to question the decisions of higher command, or of our so-called allies, indeed, questioning orders is known as mutiny, and frowned upon. But as a civilian I felt dismayed by the lack of strategic vision. I felt a keen sense of betrayal that so much blood had been spilt in vain. The Americans were finally admitting it was a massive strategic error, and comparing the humiliating end to the war on terror to the debacle of their pulling out of Vietnam. For me, it was as shameful and unnecessary as our surrender of Singapore to the Japanese in 1942. Worse, maybe. I wondered if it had always been thus. I wondered if two or three times every century, our leaders got caught with their pants down with absolutely no way of covering their arse. And whatever the cause, it was always Pvt. Tommy Atkins who paid the price, in blood. The west has fallen from grace, I thought. This isn't Viet Nam or Singapore. This is closer to the fall of Constantinople in 1453. I smiled to myself, at my ridiculous, hyperbolic state of mind. My mood reminded me of my sister-in-law's description of the period before a migraine strikes, when her brain enters a phase of expectant blankness. All there is, she explained, is a feeling of pressure somewhere at the back of the mind. She described it, eloquently, as an alert nothingness that resides until the migraine strikes, at which point everything is clarified, everything is unlocked. And this release is accompanied by an exquisite, head-destroying, earthquake of pain.

October. Three months after May left, I got a call from Tom Jarvis.

'Barrett,' he said. 'Where are you?'

'Starbucks, Clapham Junction.'

'Three minutes. I'm sending a car.'

He hung up.

I packed my rucksack, my heartbeat raised a few notches, the feeling that something, *anything* was underway. I got up and stepped out into the drizzle. A little over ninety seconds later a Range Rover pulled up and I climbed into the backseat. I was strapping on my seatbelt when the passenger up front turned to me. 'Listen up,' she said. 'Our mutual friend is holed-up in an old warehouse in Plaistow. It's empty, due for demolition, and we've cleared the area. He has explosives with him.' I nodded but said nothing. 'He's asking to speak to you,' she said.

'Me? Why?'

'That's what we've been asking ourselves for the last four months. Do you have *any* idea why he is so interested in you?'

'No.'

'You sure?'

'I don't *know* the man. I spoke to him. That's all.'

'Did he say anything?'

'Did he share his plans to cause world devastation? No.'

'You may not know him, but he knows you,' she said, like my ignorance was proof of my guilt. She'd do the inquisition proud. Just then, her phone beeped and she took a call, glancing back at me a couple of times, nodding. Finishing her call, she turned to me again. 'We rock up to the gates, a quick word with Tom, then you go in. See what he wants, come out, tell us, then we deal with it.'

We got to Plaistow in twelve minutes and, as promised, we rolled up to the rusting gates of an old factory. I got out and found myself almost dragged to a dark corner out of sightline of the factory windows. Facing me was Tom Jarvis, and I could see straight away he had his SAS head on. 'Listen to me now,' he said. 'You go in, you nod, you agree with him, you tell him anything he wants to hear. You *do not* upset him. Then you come out and tell us the lay of the land.'

'K.'

'Any questions?'

'A request.'

He looked at me keenly.

'Do not fucking shoot me when I walk out.'

He stared at me in a way that made me realise these people were not my friends. I was fully expendable, and depending on the situation, it might suit them to bag me off, along with the guy inside the factory. 'I'll keep you safe,' he said, finally. 'Just don't do anything stupid.' I was about to say something but he interrupted me, 'I *know* you can do stupid things, Mark. But not this time. No heroics, no statements, no moral high ground, please. We can't afford Sir Galahad today.' One of his crew held out a ballistic vest. I declined, turned, 'This way?'

'Hold on.' He nodded to someone sitting at the door of a comms wagon, who spoke into a handset. A moment later he said, 'Yes. Walk slowly. Stay in the light. Make yourself visible. Don't spook him.'

I did as I was told.

I walked slowly across the open space between the front gates and the building, stepped in through the doors. Found myself in the vast empty space of an old factory unit. Facing Gun Jesus.

He was merely a shadow in the darkness.

Then the shadow spoke. 'Hello Mark Barrett.' He was out of eyeline of the windows or the door, even for an infra-red. Smart.

'Hello,' I said.

I could feel him staring at me from the darkness. 'You don't remember me at all, do you?'

'Should I?'

'No. I suppose not.'

'Can I come in?' I asked. I could almost feel the red-dot sights wobbling on my back.

'Please do. You're safe.'

'I don't feel safe.'

'Safe from me,' he said. He turned and walked along a short corridor, through a room into the next. I followed. This second room was almost as dark, with corrugated iron over the windows. The wooden roof had cracks and fissures, and I was sure that if they hadn't already, the Regiment would be sending cameras filaments through some of those gaps. He caught my glance, 'They haven't had time,' he said. Smart again.

'Mind if I sit down?' I asked, pointing at a bench. Truth be told, my legs were feeling a bit wobbly. I don't mind action, but being stuck between a firing squad and an assassin has a way of making my legs shake.

'Please.'

I sat. 'They tell me you're an international assassin.' I paused. I'm not always one for great conversational openers, but this one was a zinger.

I felt rather than saw a smile.

'Why?' I asked.

'You showed me why.'

'We've never met.'

This time I saw him nod. 'We have, though you might not remember.' He took a long slow breath. 'You taught me that there has to be a price, Mark. There has to be a consequence. Otherwise, the world is chaos.'

I looked around the dim, derelict warehouse. 'You call this order?' I said. 'Or is that just when you're shooting bad guys?' He said nothing. 'You don't get to decide who are the bad guys,' I added, lamely. Truth was, he did. He had been for quite some time. He didn't answer, but sat down on an empty crate about twelve feet away. In one hand a Glock 43, in the other, fastened on by black masking tape, some sort of plastic gizmo. I watched as he attached a wire to the red plastic. At the end of the wire I saw two ammo boxes. 'It works by radio signal,' he explained, but signals can be jammed. Wire is better.' I had no doubt the ammo boxes were filled with unpleasant stuff, and I thought again of the Tyrolean hat floating to the ground, the feather smoking gently.

'Not in my world,' I told him.

'I won't trigger this until you have gone.'

'You don't strike me as suicidal.'

'This has to end.'

'Is that what you want, an end to it all?' I asked.

'Yes.'

'Then end it,' I said. 'Walk out with me. Surrender. You'll get a trial, you'll probably get life, but in this country that means fifteen years.' I guessed he was about my age, so added, 'You'll be free before you're fifty. Write a book, do the lecture circuit, set up a TikTok channel. Shit, there are ex-Mafia Capos earning millions on YouTube.'

He smiled. I could see his teeth, faintly white against the dark. 'You make it sound so easy.

'It is. You just make the decision to walk outside with me.'

'No.'

I felt frustrated. 'Why did you ask for me?'

'To remind you to deliver that package. It has sentimental value for me.'

'That's all?'

'And to say thankyou.'

'For *what*?'

He said nothing for quite a while. Just stared at me. Finally he said, 'Tell them I have four kilos of C4,' he pointed, a finger appearing out of the shadows, pointing at a box. I could see his hand and in it he held a detonator. 'I will blow myself up.'

'You don't have to.'

'You gave me a second chance.'

'I don't even know you.' I shook my head, frustrated. 'Give it up,' I repeated. 'Fifteen years in chokey then a new life as a motivational speaker.'

'I don't think I'd survive imprisonment.'

I thought for a moment. 'Yeah, well there is a good chance you'd get Epsteined.'

'A very good chance.'

'But this?'

'It will be quick.' He nodded towards the door. 'Go, Mark Barrett. Oh, and when you deliver the package, will you wait while he reads the letter?'

'Ok,' I said, only half listening.

I stood, calculated my chances of launching at him, then almost laughed, it was too far, and besides, I only wanted to get out of this awful room. If Gun Jesus wanted to give himself a C4 crucifixion, that was his lookout. I left him there in the room, my mind whirling, trying to process what he'd said, my adrenaline spiked further by the amount of C4 he had attached to a detonator strapped to his wrist. I walked back through the first room and along the short corridor, paused just short of the front door and shouted. "It's me, Barrett – I have info and I'm coming out. Don't fucking shoot me!"

I heard a voice shouting the usual, "Come out, Hands up" etc. and I stepped back into the light. I got halfway across the courtyard before I was tackled to the ground, cuffed and dragged around the corner to the command vehicle, and allowed to stand again.

'Get these fucking cuffs *off* me,' I told Jarvis who was waiting there expectantly.

He took out a knife and split the flexi-cuffs, releasing my hands. 'Spill,' he said.

I saw a Chinese guy standing beside him. 'Who's this?'

'A friend of ours,' he said.

'I seriously doubt it,' I said.

'*Mark*...' he began but I interrupted.

'Four kilos of C4, or thereabouts. He has the detonator taped to his hand and it's on a dead-man's trigger. He dies, or lets go, and it all goes up.'

'Hardwired?' the Chinese said.

'Very,' I said, looking at Tom.

'Is he going to surrender?'

'I think he came here to die.'

'Fuck.'

Tom jogged over to the comms van and spoke to the operator. The Chinese guy was still standing beside me, he said nothing, but studied me for a long moment. 'Mark Barrett,' he said, finally.

'Yes.'

He pointed two fingers towards his own eyes, then turned his hand to point a forefinger at me. 'Always,' he said quietly. 'We watch you.'

I was tempted to put his teeth through the back of his skull, in fact I was lining him up for the Kebab Special when Jarvis walked back to us and, sensing the tension, put his hand on my arm and guided me away, 'Ignore him, he's all...'

The world turned white.

And silent.

Then we were floating through the air.

I hit the ground hard, with Jarvis' elbow hitting me in the chest first and Tom himself following a millisecond later, the fall knocking the wind out of me, the elbow breaking some ribs, and Tom's weight just making the entire idea of breathing unpleasant. I lay there for a while, in the dark, ears ringing, and when I did try to breath, an extremely sharp pain in my side where Tom's elbow had speared my short rib persuaded me to stop.

'You ok?' I heard a voice.

I took a conscious effort to inhale. 'Squared away,' I replied, my voice a whisper, because that was all the wind I could muster to speak. I felt a hand grab my wrist and pull me to a standing position, which was agony, and I doubled over in pain. Someone squirted water in my face, staring into my eyes and speaking words I couldn't hear. It was the Comms guy. Turns out he was in the van when the warehouse blew and, though the van had turned over with the blast, and he had blood running from both ears, nevertheless had immediately begun triaging the injured. My eyes almost clear, still doubled over with pain, I saw Tom dusting himself down, the Chinese guy was already on the phone, filming what was left of the warehouse.

'Mark?'

I turned, it was Ruby. She must have been somewhere close. She looked panicked by whatever state I was in. 'Hey,' I said, trying but failing to stand up straight.

'You look like shit. Come with me.'

She led, half dragged me away from the scene of devastation and bundled me into a Range Rover where she checked me over, noting my busted side. I heard her tell the driver to get us to hospital in a voice that would have done an RSM proud.

I blacked out.

When I woke again, I could hardly breathe, but I had to ask, 'Gun Jesus?'

Ruby closed down the phone conversation she was having and turned to me, a look of real concern on her face. She nodded. 'Was anyone there with him?'

'No, just him.'

'Well then, it's over. He's gone.'

I felt like someone had inserted a porcupine into my chest cavity, and then I coughed, which brought me a world of sharp, burning agony, and brought up a whole lot of blood too. Ruby leaned forward so she could see my face, which was somewhere near my knees at this point. 'Move your arse, Sergeant! We need to be there in under three minutes.'

'On it,' he said, switching on the sirens and flashers. I felt the car surge forward. I coughed up more blood, 'Ruby,' I said...

'Your short rib punctured the left lung, which would have collapsed, but for the fact it was filled with blood.' The doctor looked at his notes and read on. 'Then you got an infection. And you died a couple of times. But now,' he gave a slightly ghoulish smile, 'You're on the road to recovery.'

I nodded, feeling heavy and sleepy from whatever drug cocktail they'd been pumping into my arm from a bag hanging on a wire frame beside me. 'How long before I can leave?' I whispered, my throat hoarse from lack of use.

'She said that'd be the first thing you ask. So, I'd say, as soon as you can walk the length of the ward, twice, unaided, I'll think about signing you off.'

'Right, I said, trying to lever myself out of bed. 'Let's get...'

I opened my eyes.

It struck me that some time had passed since my conversation with the doctor.

Ruby sat in front of me.

'You daft twat,' she said. 'You pulled out half the stitches trying to get out of the bed. Blood all over. Fucking maniac.'

'Did I die again,' I said, with an attempt at a winning smile.

She grimaced. 'Give yourself a week, at least, please, before you attempt to parachute off the bed.'

'K,' I said.

'You're a fucking lunatic, Mark. But that's why I love you.'

I raised an eyebrow.

She said, 'Like a brother. A mad fucking brother.' She added, 'However, as representative of the government, I'm authorised to say that if there's anything you'd like, let me know.' She laid a phone on the bed beside me. 'It's got my direct number. *Don't* use it for watching porn, cos I can do without the hassle, and your lungs can't manage the exertion right now.' Then she stood and left, or at least I think she did, I was asleep before she reached the door. Whatever drugs they gave me, my dreams were vivid, and some cold part of my mind tracked them, knowing that they'd get less crazy as I healed. And they did. I spent the next few days sleeping a lot, waking, eating ice cream, mashed potato, and at one point I woke to find a nurse cleaning my teeth. Which begged other questions. And that did wake me. 'I need the toilet,' I whispered.

The nurse paused from scrubbing my incisors and looked down at me. 'You could do with a shave too, my hand is raw.'

'Where am I?"
'Military hospital, Mitcham.'
'There is no mili... ah, right,' I said. 'Can I sit up?'
'Sure, but take it easy.'
She went to help me but I managed to sit up myself,
carefully, avoiding most of the pain. There was a drip
attached to my arm, and a line that went to a bag on
a trolley. It felt like my entire life consisted of drips
into my arm, and at that point, it pretty much did.
Together we made it out of the bed though, and she
held my arm and pushed the bag-on-a-trolley, as we
walked to the toilet. 'Want me to come in with you?'
'Tempting,' I said, 'But I think I'll manage.'
'Don't lock the door,' she said as I went inside. 'If you
collapse and we have to kick the door down, I'll miss
a promotion.'
Army nurse, I thought.
I locked the door.

Six days later I managed to walk the length of the
ward, twice, and was allowed to leave. My ribs were
itching like crazy, but scratching hurt more than the
itching itched, and my lung was healing though my
breathing was still a bit laboured. However, I was
going to survive. It turned out that there were only
three injuries from the explosion, not including the
tattered remains of the person inside the
warehouse. The Chinese guy hadn't known it, but a
fragment of wood from a doorframe had pierced his
liver, he thought the blow had just hit his body
armour and bounced off, but it had gone through

and, while on his phone to the authority back in Beijing, he collapsed. No one noticed at first, there was a lot going on, but eventually a squaddie tripped over him and alerted the medics. The comms expert had both eardrums blown, and though he'd regained most of his hearing, he wouldn't be working comms for a while. Apart from that everyone else was shaken but ok.

The Chinese Premier cancelled his visit. Explanations were given, diplomatic apologies accepted, and over a few days the proposed visit of the leader of the new world order was memory-holed. By the time I returned to my flat, three weeks after I'd left it, the cancelled visit of the Chinese premier was forgotten, and a mysterious gas main explosion in some abandoned south London warehouse occupied no more than two lines in a google search. The news cycle had turned and then turned again.

A week later, I was in the basement when I heard a knock on the window. I wiped excess oil from my hands and opened the door to the yard. 'Hey,'

It was Millie, my upstairs neighbour. 'Where've you been?' quickly followed by, 'Shit you look awful, Mark.'

Millie on the other hand looked and smelled lovely, healthy and young. All the things I didn't. 'Want to come in for a coffee?' I said.

'Aint got time,' she said, 'You forgot this, been holding onto it for weeks,' holding out a package.

I stared at it, knowing what it was but not sure that I wanted to accept it, after the events of the last few weeks. But she kept on holding it out until I took it.

'Thanks,' I said.

'Well, got to go.'

'You got a date?' she looked very smart.

'Interview.'

'Well, break a leg,' I said.

'In these heels? Very likely,' she said with a laugh. She had a nice smile. Friendly and warm. Stop it, Barrett, I told myself. 'I have to go,' she said, and left me standing on the step.

I went back inside, closed the door and stared at the package. I went upstairs to call Greener, decided to email him as I couldn't face a conversation with my oldest friend at that moment. I knew what he'd say. But in the space of two hours I got two calls. The first was from Ruby, as I washed up in the bathroom, grinding away the oil with a bristle brush that seemed to take off the skin while somehow leaving a black stain intact. 'Hey gorgeous,' she said. 'We found him.'

'Found who?'

'The man who detonated a small part of south London. There wasn't much left but what we did find, we ran a DNA check. Turns out he was German. Ex-SF. Became political a few years ago, went awol.'

'What was he called?' I turned of the tap, dried my hands, each finger in turn, as I listened. I wanted to put a name to that quiet, softly spoken face.

'Drechsler. Bruno Drechsler,' she said. 'A seriously nasty piece of work. Murderer. Torturer. Far right. Or far left. Pretty much the same anyway.'

I asked her to spell his name, walked into the kitchen and jotted it down on a notepad when she did, but I was thinking, he didn't come across as nasty. Deranged, sure, but, well, what did I know.

'The Germans were tracking Drechsler until a couple of weeks ago, when he fell off the map.'

'And he ended up here.'

'Yes.'

'So that's it,' I said. 'He's gone. All is well with the world.' I felt a little flat.

She laughed. 'It'll make your life easier,' she said. 'No more being arrested by the Spesh.'

'Hey, don't knock it, my bank balance is happy. But what about your life. Will it be easier now?'

'That would be a big No,' she said, her tone growing serious. 'The events of the last few months have made the world an extremely unsafe place. And God save us from the intervention of fucking liberal do-gooders with money to waste, they cause more trouble than any warlord or failed state.'

'You'll survive,' I said.

'I'd like to think so. Anyhow, just thought I'd let you know.'

'K, speak soon.'

I ended the call and put down the phone. Went back into the bathroom and finished cleaning beneath my fingernails with a small bristle brush bought for that very purpose. I looked in the fridge with a plan to make myself some lunch, but I saw that after a week or two away from home my fridge was sadly depleted of good stuff. I grabbed my wallet and rucksack and took a walk to my local Tesco Express, where I stocked up on food, cleaning products and some air freshener as per the permanent, but unspoken unspoken instructions from my sister-in-law. Personal admin never sleeps. As I stood in the queue for the single checkout with my shopping, I got the second call. It was Greener.

'Barrett,' he said. 'What's with the email? You avoiding me, man?'

'Always, Greens, you're a bad influence. What's up?'

'That name you gave me, I think I've narrowed it down. My cousin knows a guy with that name, Afghan refugee, came here about four years ago, runs a little cafe in Canning Town.' He gave me an address. I took out my notebook and jotted it down. 'Hold on,' I said, unloading my small trolley full of food onto the conveyor belt. 'Yeah,' I said, finally. 'Thanks for that.'

He said, 'You sound down, man.'

'I'm at Tesco Express.'

'Same thing,' he laughed.

'I've had an interesting time,' I said, phone jammed between ear as I bagged off the goods the checkout girl rang through. 'I'm looking forward to a long period of boring.'

'You need to drop an anchor, Mark,' he said. 'You need to find a safe harbor and rest a while. You been bouncing through life like a pinball.'

'Got any more metaphors you can mix on my behalf?'

He laughed again. 'You know it, don't you? I mean, what's happened to you and Beth?' And when I stayed silent he said, 'I thought you two were going to make it work this time?' He said, 'I'm not scolding you, Mark, I've got your back, mate. I'm just concerned, at our age we should be putting down roots.'

'I know, thanks, G.'

'Come on down some time, we'll get drunk, set the world to rights.'

'Will do.'

'Seriously, mate. Do.'

He hung up.

I pocketed my phone and picked up my now full shopping bag. When I got home, I unloaded my food, made myself a cheese omelet and a fresh pot of coffee. After I'd eaten and washed up, I sat down. I stared at the address Greener had given me. Maybe now I could carry out this one final job on behalf of Mr. Herr. Mr. Drechsler. The mission-orientated serial killer formerly known as Gun Jesus. or whatever he was called. All the strands had come together. All I had to do was tie them into a bow. I pulled on my jacket, tucked the package into a pocket, left my basement flat and walked to the tube.

The Jubilee line took me to Canning Town. I took a chance at the zebra crossing, and jogged across the dual, walked beneath the flyover and followed my nose 'til I got to Barking Road. A few minutes more and I found the cafe, a tiny little place lodged between Cohen's Optometrists and Canning Town Turkish barbers. There was a sign, but it was in Farsi. This wasn't the fabled cockney-sparrer East End of world war 2 era "Britain Can Take It" and it wasn't Ye Olde Englande of the Henry the Eighth, history books and Peasant Revolts, this was the multi-culti world of today. More than half the population derived from elsewhere and, as I looked around, I realised that I was, in fact, something a racial minority. Maybe I could cash in my victim card. I went to the hand-

painted red door and pushed. Inside smelled of spices and coffee, and a hint of testosterone. The kid behind the counter was no more than thirteen, but he eyed me with suspicion. 'Help you?' he asked.
'I'm looking for,' I held up the package, showed him the picture.
The kid stared at it. 'Who's it from?'
'I dunno. I was just asked to deliver it. Is he here?'
The kid shouted something in Farsi, while staring at me. A moment or two later a man of about forty came hobbling out from the back, and he shouted something at the kid. He came to the counter and smiled. 'Can I help you?'
'I'm looking for Zemar Ridai'
Suspicion flickered across his smile. 'That is me.'
I held up the package and said, 'A man asked me to deliver this to you.'
'Oh.'
He took it and looked at it. I remembered Drechsler's request and waited as the man shouted to the kid, who came back into the front and took it from him, picked up a small, sharp knife and opened it. The kid read something out that I couldn't understand, and the man nodded, 'That is me,' he acknowledged again, and he flicked through the half dozen photographs inside, his expression moving swiftly through a number of moods in only seconds. Then he said something to the kid, who began reading whatever the letter said in the man's own language, I heard my name mentioned at one point. The man listened intently. Glancing at me once or twice, his

faced changed as the kid read, moving from dark suspicion to a nodding understanding, and then to becoming visibly moved with emotion. The kid paused to look at me as he read, hostility changing to something else that I couldn't quite place. When he was finished, the man said to the kid, 'Read it again, in English. Read it please.'

The kid, nodded. "To Mr. Ridai You will not remember me, but we met once, briefly, across a battlefield. I was injured, a Dutch soldier, shot in the chest, and dying, and you too were injured and dying, your leg destroyed by a grenade. We were enemies in a war that neither of us began.' The kid paused to take a deep breath, wiped his eye, then continued. "The man who delivered this letter does not know its contents, but he is the man who saved both our lives. He is the helicopter pilot who risked his life to save me, and then risked his life again to save you, an enemy combatant. His name is Mark Barrett." The kid looked at me and I confirmed this with a nod.

The kid read on. "We will never meet, sadly, and we only spoke a few times in the hospital ward before we were separated, the attached photographs are of us in that short time, but I never forgot you or the things you talked about: your plans for the future, the family you wanted to join in England, your wife who died giving birth to your daughter. All the dreams and all the memories a man should have but that would have ended on a hillside but for one man who chose to save you, and me. I wanted you to meet the man to whom we both owe our lives." The kid stopped reading out loud, mumbled a few things as he read something, then reached into the envelope and took out a scrap of material and handed it to me. Still holding the letter, he said, 'Uncle told me this story but I never believed it. I never believed an English soldier would do that for an Afghan.'

I was only half listening, it was too much to take in all at once; my mind was back in the air over foreign lands, hearing a warning not to approach, hearing the cries over the radio of a troop of Dutch peacekeepers pinned down in a crossfire, hearing my gunner yelling, 'Don't you do it, Barrett! Don't you fuckin' put us down there. Don't do it!'

But I'd done it.

And here was the proof.

I looked at the scrap of material in my hand. A uniform badge, bayonets crossed over a fusilard, gold over black and green. Dutch Special Forces. One edge of the material was darkened with an old stain that might have been blood. I looked up at the man as he came round from behind the counter, tears in his eyes. His limp was caused by a prosthetic lower leg, though he moved with the ease of someone who had worn it for some years, someone with indomitable spirit. Someone with fire. Without a word he embraced me and he hugged me tight, saying some words that I could not understand. He turned to the kid who took out his phone and motioned to me. The kid took a photo of us both, together. I saw it later, and I was smiling, though I can't remember doing so. I do remember the kid telling me that his uncle had a new wife and two small children, who would not have been in the world but for me, and he had a life in England and a business, this business, and he was working hard for his family was thriving, and that he, the kid, was working hard here in the cafe, and in school, and that the family were going to prosper, because of me. It was too much to take in. I hugged the man in return. He smelled of food and fire and life, and I held this man whose life I'd saved, and forced back the tears. Eventually the man told his nephew to make us coffee and we sat down at a table drinking sweet black coffee that made my heart race. Maybe it wasn't just the coffee. I smiled, I chatted, but I couldn't help but zone out. It was all too much. Soldiers tend to remember the bodies they've made, not the people they've saved. I sat at the table with this vigorous man, a man with children and a business and a life, and I couldn't compute the situation. My head felt fuzzy. After a few more minutes, I made my goodbyes, shook hands, took another embrace across the table, almost spilling my coffee, and then I stood and went to the counter, left my card the kid, and then with one last nod to the man, I left the cafe and stepped back out into the world. It was raining. And the rain was welcome. I walked back towards the tube station, struggling to breathe correctly, my throat constricting with emotion. I thought of Mr. Herr telling me 'You're a good man, Mark Barrett.' I heard him telling me I was worth more than I thought I was. I knew that on this occasion he was right. But I smiled too, almost laughed out loud. Because I knew he wasn't Drechsler. Drechsler was German. The man I'd rescued on that Afghan hillside was Dutch. The badge he'd left me was Dutch Special Forces.

He wasn't dead.

I realised, with absolute certainty, he'd faked it. He'd performed a bait and switch, and everyone had fallen for it. Gun Jesus had done what it said on the tin, he'd died to make the world a better place, and now he was alive again.

It was still raining as I entered the tube station. Not heavy; just a low, constant, grey London rain, and the passing traffic hummed with the sound of wheels shedding water. But my mood had lifted, despite the grey skies. He'd done it, I thought. Somehow, he'd fooled everyone into thinking he was someone else. Someone who was now officially dead. 'I wanted to show the world that there is always a price to be paid,' he'd told me. 'And now I want to retire,' he'd said. 'I've done enough. I want to stop this life.'

And he had.

I was smiling when I reached the platform. I was smiling for a wounded Dutchman who'd got a second chance, and used it to rid the world of some of the greater evils. I was smiling for an Afghan who'd lived and prospered. And I was smiling for myself because, somehow, amidst the recklessness and chaos that was most of my life, I'd done a good thing. And there were other things I could do, to make the world a little better. I thought of a tiny, vulnerable girl, trying to make her peace with a dangerous, unforgiving world, a girl I'd treat with less than care. Perhaps she might forgive me, I thought. Perhaps not. I could only try. I dug through my wallet until I found her business card – the only details on it were a name, a number and a hand-drawn smiley face – then I took out my phone and began dialing.

Mark Barrett will return in **Über Lord**

'Mr. Barrett?'

I turned to see a smartly dressed woman standing beside me. I'd been enjoying the relative peace of central London in the sun, sitting at a cafe table on the river at Southwark, my back to the re-creation of Shakespeare's Globe theatre. It was a warm summer day with no wind, I'd been daydreaming and had filtered out the background noise of traffic and the faint rumble coming from the nearby railway lines. I stood, 'Yes, that's me.'

We shook hands. Her grip was dry and firm. 'My name is Jane Charter, I work for Mr. Lord.'

Tim Lord, I thought.

The Über-Lord.

Prior to this meeting, a brief but enlightening google search had revealed that Tim Lord was not only a super-geek billionaire, but a venture-philanthropist, a jiu-jitsu black belt and expert rock climber. He was the English Elon Musk, people said, a European Tai Pan, that he owned most of Luxembourg, he owned nothing, he was the 21st Century Thomas Edison. The next article on the search engine revealed he was a vegan. The one after that stated he ate only meat. He slept three hours a night. He only slept on Sundays. He only slept with supermodels. He was gay. He was straight. He was a hermaphrodite. He worked for the Russians. He worked for the Chinese. The factoid-replete articles were endless and mostly contradictory, and there were any number of conspiracy theories attached to each and every one of these debatable facts. He was building an underwater city. He was planning to live on Mars. He was engaged on reducing world hunger, world population, and world debt. And for each of those theories, the opposite also existed. I wondered how many of these untruths were planted by his rivals and, indeed, how many he'd planted himself. Tim Lord was one of the neo-feudalists who'd arrived not on the back of a destrier, dressed in mail and armed with mace and flail, but who'd via the internet and the stock exchange, armed with charm and mystery money and complete belief in himself and his own destiny.

Jane Charter sat down opposite me.

She placed her phone on the table, lining it up perfectly with the straight-edge of the pattern carved into the wood, and opened her briefcase. I sat back down and waited. As she took out a folder, she was speaking, 'Mr. Lord has a contract that he would like you to undertake. He is currently working on a project for which there are five separate elements; each one is being developed independently, in hermetically sealed IT units across greater London.' She opened the folder on the desk. 'Mr. Lord would like to put you on a retainer for the four months.' She looked at me. 'You would be on call day and night. As and when each independent project reaches fruition, he would like you to collect it and deliver it.'

'Do you have the addresses?' I asked.

'You will be given the addresses as we move forward.'

Her hair was pulled back as tightly as her delivery of the lines she was speaking. I looked at the first sheet of paper, and saw that the money was good. I'd be on call 24/7 until the autumn. Ok, I thought. For that rate, I can be on call.

'If the contract is finished within the four-week period, you will still get the full stipend, as agreed,' she said, pointing to the figure I'd just clocked. I wondered what underwear she was wearing. Any girl who used the word *stipend* with a straight face just had to be wild in bed.

Silk, I decided.

She pushed forward a sheaf of papers. 'We need you to sign an NDA before I can give you any further details.'

This gave me pause. 'I don't sign NDAs,' I said.

She too paused. Her eyebrows were raised in a question mark.

Quietly, I repeated what I said.

'Then we have a problem,' she said.

'I don't give up information on my clients, or the work I do for them,' I said. 'Not ever. Not to anyone. Unless they involve me in something illegal, in which case the deal is off. My relationship with the client is absolutely discrete. Signing an NDA would suggest that my silence can be bought.'

'Suggest to who?' she asked.

'To me.'

'Can you be bought?' she asked.

'No.'

She stayed quiet for a moment, her eyes glancing up and to the left to one side. I realised she was listening to someone speaking in an earpiece, though it was so small I hadn't noticed it up until this point. She nodded imperceptibly, then looked up at me, began tidying away her papers. 'It really is standard practice,' she told me.

'I know,' I said.

'You must lose lots of work.'

'It's my operating system,' I said.

She raised an eyebrow, giving me slightly less than one eighth of a smile. Mentally, I added to myself, *black* silk. And I knew I'd never find out.

Other novels in the Mark Barrett series:

NQA

.50 Cal

Spenderella

.

Printed in Great Britain
by Amazon